Saving Lives Unintended Timing

Saving Lives Unintended Timing

Thistle Rose

Strategic Book Publishing and Rights Co.

Strategic Book Publishing and Rights Co.
12620 FM 1960, Suite A4-507
Houston, TX 77065
www.sbpra.com

ISBN: 978-1-62516-860-3

Dedication

To my friend Caz, who has encouraged and listened to my mad ramblings for years, giving me hope.

Also to my two boys, William and Daniel, who have supported and come on this journey in life with me.

Prologue

The assassin climbed in through the upstairs window and crept downstairs to the kitchen. He took the package out of his rucksack. His breathing was heavy, and the adrenaline pulsing through his body caused tiny beads of sweat to form above his eyebrows. He attached the package to the boiler and went back to the upstairs window he had come through. On the way he noted a few candles and crystals scattered on shelves.

He hoped the society had gotten their information correct this time and that the women living in the house were indeed witches. Candles and crystals were nothing but fancy decorations to most people these days.

Now that the bomb was set, he headed back to the unit to see his commander and his son Joe.

Chapter One

1985

Janet

After spending an extra half hour to get her overexcited girls to go to sleep, Janet was exhausted and annoyed at her sister Hettie and her mother for filling her daughters' heads with silly ideas and stories about the women in their family. They had taken it upon themselves to gossip to Aine, her eldest, who enjoyed sports and had short strawberry blonde hair, tomboyish features, and wild green eyes, and Anchorette, her youngest, who, like their Grandmama Hartwood, loved to cook and sample the goods of labor and had grayish-blue eyes and caramel blonde hair that was quite long.

Before the girls were born, Grandmama Hartwood knew that they, like all the women in the family, would have a birthmark. Aine's was a circle about the size of a twopence piece with eight smaller dots around it, and Anchorette's was shaped like the number eight with three small circles above it. Both birthmarks were on the ankle, with Aine's on her left and Anchorette's on her right. Grandmama Hartwood, much to Janet's annoyance, was a practicing Wiccan, and so was her sister, who had quite happily followed suit.

Janet could not fathom how she had grown up in such a dysfunctional family. Her daughters had been told that they possessed the ability to heal much more quickly than average. Aine once told Janet about a neat trick Aunt Hettie had shown her: Aine had accidentally sliced the tip of her finger while making their sandwiches at lunchtime, and Aunt Hettie gently blew upon the cut and then showed Aine that the cut had stopped bleeding and was already healed. Anchorette had not seen this and so was slightly sceptical. Grandmama Hartwood was slightly displeased with Aunt Hettie but had, however, continued to tell them both about a gift, a special talent, that they would both develop when they came of age during puberty. Anchorette was slightly confused, being only eight, but Aine, being ten, knew a little about being a female and was very excited. This had rubbed off onto Anchorette, and this was why it had been difficult to get them off to sleep.

Janet was sitting at the kitchen table with a cup of tea when the doorbell rang. Given that it was half past nine in the evening, Janet wondered who could be calling upon her at such a late time. She checked to make sure the security chain was still in place before turning the latch to open the door just a fraction of an inch.

"Good evening, I am sorry it is late, but could my colleague and I please have a word with you, Mrs. Hews?" It was PC Hampton and his colleague, WPC Sprite. Janet knew that nothing good would come of this. She had grown up in the small town and so knew Hampton and Sprite from her school days, and remembered when Mark Hampton pulled the red ribbons from her pigtails in first grade.

"Of course," Janet said as she closed the front door to unhook the chain. Once they were in she closed the front door again and showed them into the front room.

"Would you like a cup of tea or coffee? The kettle is just boiled," Janet said as she offered them seats. She really didn't like Mark Hampton, but her mother had always insisted on house politeness.

"WPC Sprite will make us all a fresh cup. Please sit down," PC Hampton said as he took up a seat on one of the empty armchairs. Janet sat down very awkwardly at the edge of the sofa. "When was the last time you had contact with or saw your mother and sister Janet?" PC Hampton asked.

"Just a while ago. I picked up the girls from Mum's place, as they had spent all day there. In fact I have only just gotten them settled down. Why, has something happened?" Janet asked the question but did not really want to hear the answer.

PC Hampton took a moment before answering. "I'm sorry to say this, but there has been some kind of explosion at your mother's house. Your mother and sister Hettie were in at the time and had no chance of escape. I'm sorry for your loss. Will your husband be home soon?"

Janet tilted her head to one side as if thinking would make this news any clearer. What happened after was a blur for Janet. The house became very loud, with a scream repeating over and over exactly the same thing: "Oh my god, oh my, oh my god, not Mum, not Hettie."

PC Hampton looked to the floor. WPC Sprite came back in from the kitchen and sat next to Janet, putting her arm around her. Janet's screams and tears were muffled by her arm.

PC Hampton cleared his throat and spoke again after Janet had regained a little composure. "I know this is difficult, but were there any problems in the house between you and your sister or your mother?" Janet shook her head and mumbled no. "Can you remember what time you and your daughters left?" PC Hampton asked.

"We came back at around four, as I had to get them some dinner. How did this happen?" Janet asked.

WPC Sprite passed Janet one of the cups and said, "Here, drink this sweet tea. It helps with the shock."

Janet looked up at the female policewoman, trying so hard to remember her first name, her hand shaking and spilling tea down her leg.

"Where is your husband?" WPC Sprite asked. Janet took a moment to realize she was alone.

"He works offshore on an oil rig. He spends three weeks on and three weeks off. He only went back two days ago."

"Do you know of anyone who would want to harm your mother or sister?" PC Hampton asked. Again Janet mumbled no, shaking her head as if an answer would come to mind.

"Mummy, Mummy, Mummy, is it true, is it true that Grandmama and Aunt Hettie are dead?" Aine asked as she came running in, screaming questions at her mum.

"Yes it is, honey. Were you listening in?" Janet asked, slightly annoyed at Aine for getting out of her bed and coming down the stairs.

"No, Gran told me in a dream. She told us to be careful and to be strong and that she loves us," Aine sobbed.

Chapter Two

Present Day

Anchorette

Drip, drip, clickety-clack, clickety-clack was all that Anchorette heard. The rain was beating on the window and the gutters were in need of being cleaned. She could hear the wheels of the coal buckets on their way to the docks where they would be loaded up and shipped off.

The week had been filled heavily with rain, and the weekend was not looking any different. The day was gray, wet, and cold, and the sound she had woken up to was that of her loving husband of four years. Joe had been out the night before at the snooker hall. He didn't play professionally; he just wished he did. It would be an easier way to make to a living, not having to drive an hour to work and be stuck in a job that made him tired and ratty. But they were committed to each other and had been dating since Anchorette's second year of high school. He had walked into her life just as her sister had walked out with her drugs. Childhood sweethearts—everyone in town knew it. Now they had a mortgage on a three-bedroom house in a good area. The neighbours were good and the street was clean despite the amount of dirt that came from the docks with the offloading; no littering or having to concentrate on where to put your feet for fear of a dog having fouled the street.

Anchorette gently got out of bed as to not wake Joe up. It was Saturday, and she had work in ninety minutes. As she went to the bathroom she could hear Keith just waking up; he was only six months old but was already sleeping all through the night.

Anchorette got dressed and went to Keith's bedroom door, where she was greeted by a meow from Minstral. He rubbed his body up against her leg and flicked it with a light swish of his tail. Anchorette bent down and stroked his back. "I shall get you some food in a moment or two," Anchorette said as she entered Keith's bedroom. She went over to Keith's wardrobe, picked out clothes for the day, and grabbed his bag of nappies and wipes to clean and change him on the mat. Keith was all smiles. He was quite a calm baby and it never took her long to get him ready, but she had just enough time to fix his breakfast and let the cats outside, though she doubted they'd go out given that the rain was now coming down hard and fast.

In the kitchen Anchorette flicked on the switch. She would make Joe a wake-up cup of coffee and take it to him after she had given Keith his breakfast, which looked and smelled horrible, but Keith seemed to like it and he ate it all the same. Anchorette knew she could grab food at work while the night shift worker handed over the details of who had tried to escape during the night or who had tried to flood one of the bathrooms. These reports always amused her.

Anchorette had worked in a residential nursing home before having Keith, and they had been glad to have her back. The job involved running around and changing the residents' bedding and listening to their complaints about their next-door neighbour keeping them up for most the night by flushing the toilet in their en-suite bathroom. To Anchorette it was like a version of the living dead. Some of the residents were sane, but some of them just had way too much money and had lost their common sense—or any other sense, for that matter—and should have been locked in the psychiatric ward a long time ago; the shame of that, however, would have been way too much for the upper-class people and their pride. Anchorette's parents had said that if either of them were in any way disturbed, she should drive them to the front door of Nut House Valley, ring the damn bell, and leave them there. Did that make her sound like a cruel and heartless daughter who did not care? Hell no, because Anchorette, much to her disgust, had had this discussion years ago after Aine had chosen to leave the family home. Her parents had told her that if they started to lose their minds, she was to shoot them both. While that was tempting, she couldn't fulfill that request even if it were required; she did not want to spend any time at Her Majesty's pleasure. Anchorette felt that if you were going to commit a crime, you should at least make sure that you don't get caught. She, however, had been too chicken to commit such an act on occasions when her mother had pushed her to a blind rage, and she also was a really, really bad liar, so bad that she looked worse than a deer caught in headlights. Aine, on the other hand, could have lied at the drop of a hat and never blinked.

While walking up the stairs with Keith in one arm and Joe's morning cup of coffee in the other hand, she wondered how people could lie to one another. It was moments like that when Anchorette realized just how much she loved Joe, even when he smelled of stale smoke and beer.

While placing the coffee on the bedside table and letting Keith attempt to climb over Joe to wake him up, Anchorette heard another meow. It was not a normal meow; this one was from another cat, also completely black but of Siamese descent. Her meow sounded quite different. It was a meow Anchorette loved and Joe hated, especially when he had a hangover. Joe grumbled his way out from under the duvet to ask why the cat had to make that noise, but he was silenced by Keith putting a finger up his nose. Keith was certainly getting faster and exploring with a lot more confidence.

Joe saw that Anchorette was wearing her uniform and frowned. He didn't like it when she had to go to work, but bills had to be paid and every penny counted. Keith was growing so fast. Anchorette noticed that he was in need of some new sleep suits; his toes were poking out of holes in the feet. Janet had warned her that when Keith learned to walk, the holes would move from his toes to his knees and he would scrape his skin while crawling and be covered in bloody grass stains. Anchorette shuddered at the thought of her son being hurt; even taking him to the doctor to get his vaccinations had been difficult.

Anchorette had always had a phobia for needles, and her mother had ridiculed her as a child for not being brave. Aine, however, had always been praised for not crying or screaming when being jabbed. It later turned out that this was not such a good thing, as Aine developed an addiction to drugs, and rumors of her using crack had been whispered more than once. That, and rumors of people's homes being broken into and items missing.

Joe didn't like Aine much but tolerated her because of Anchorette. They had not seen her for almost four years. Anchorette guessed that Aine had left because their mum and dad had each other and she had Joe, so there was not much for her to hang around for. Anchorette and Joe heard on the grapevine every now and then that she was living in a hostel or that she had been seen by one of her friends on a night out in the city incredibly high. Although people in the town knew that she and her family had tried to do their best by her, it still didn't stop the whispering behind their backs. It had been tough at first but Anchorette had carried on, and Joe found it easiest out of them all.

Anchorette looked down at Midnight, who was still meowing, and noticed that she had run a ladder through her tights. Oh well, it was her last pair. She would have to put that on her shopping list for Monday's trip into town. She was sure the matron would give her a warning look about not complying with the dress code.

While removing her tights, Anchorette said, "Joe, honey, I have to go now. Your breakfast is ready. Keith has had his already—he just needs some juice when you're ready. The cats have been fed and I'm now running late, so a quick kiss and then I have to go, okay?"

Joe looked up at Anchorette. "Yeah, okay, see you later I guess. I might go into town today to take Keith to see his grandparents." His attention went back to Keith.

"Sounds like a plan," Anchorette said, all chipper. She kissed Keith and Joe and then left the bedroom. She bounced down the stairs and out the door, picking up her umbrella for the quick, brisk walk to work. She was in real need of toast and a glass of orange juice before she sat in to hear the details of the night shift.

Chapter Three

Anchorette

The air was damp and the wind was blustery. She struggled with the umbrella; it would not open up properly and damn well nearly took the top part of her scalp away with it. She gave up and found a bin on the way and dumped it in aggressively, but the hook on the handle got caught on her coat. Anchorette finally succeeded in leaving it behind after a little swearing and enduring an odd look from a man walking his dog; they both looked a lot drier than she did. She walked a little farther up a street and turned down an alleyway. She passed the local police station, turned right at the next corner, and then turned left to walk up the sloped drive to the main entrance. She heard her name from behind one of the many trees that stood along the stone wall that lined the drive. It sounded faint and unsure, and at first she was concerned that she was about to be mugged.

The voice came again, this time a little more certain. "Anchorette, how you doing?" It took her a second or two to match the voice with the face that was coming out from a gap between the wall and the tree. The voice sounded familiar but a little unsteady and unsure, and the face looked familiar but thin and gaunt. The woman's hair looked wild and wet from the rain, like she had been hiding behind the tree for some time, and considering her appearance, Anchorette's gut instinct of being mugged could have been plausible. The woman looked like someone you would have walked past on the street, thinking that she didn't deserve a chance. That person, however, was Aine, and when Aine saw Anchorette's face, she must have been going through a whole array of expressions, because by the time she had finally settled on relief Aine looked all defensive.

Anchorette went over to hug Aine, but Aine backed away, clearly hurt. "I went to see Mum and Dad this morning," she said. "They were not at all welcoming. They told me to go away, that they were not prepared to give me any more money and that I was on my own. I didn't even get to explain to them why I was there. I have come back because I need help. I know that I can't do this on my own any—" Aines voice weakened, tears ran down her already wet face, and her knees buckled. Anchorette ran to help her to the ground. As she put her hand around Aine, Anchorette could feel how thin she was. "He died right next to me. I didn't even realize that he had gone, he looked so happy. He just looked like he was sleeping. Until I saw the bruising." Aine sobbed into Anchorette's arm.

"Who died?" Anchorette asked, wiping the tears from Aine's face with a tissue that she had gotten out of her coat pocket. She seriously smelled really bad, like a creature of the night, bad enough that she looked like one!

"My boyfriend, Brett. He died a week ago. I have been walking around on the streets since then. I couldn't go back home. I just grabbed my gear and have been walking around, sleeping in shelters and hostels when I can get a bed for the night. I know what I have to do but I can't go it alone. I'm so scared. I need help. I need your help. Please, I know I have said this loads of time before, but this time I really mean it. I have to get clean. I can't do this no more," she said, hiccupping and sobbing. Anchorette looked at Aine and knew that she had hit rock bottom.

Anchorette had to help, but how? Ask Joe to fund her to go to rehab? No, he would never do that. He would much rather have burned cheques. He would be just like their parents and tell Anchorette that Aine was not worth it.

Think, girl, think. How could she help Aine do this? It was not that Anchorette was lacking in experience of this kind, really. Janet and Dave had been the ones to handle Aine's addictions years ago, as Anchorette had been too young to do it. Could she be strong enough to do it now?

"Take it that you don't believe me, either?" Aine said, her voice defensive.

Anchorette looked down at her and realized that she must have taken long in thinking. Anchorette said, "It's not that I don't believe you. I just don't know what I can do to help. I mean, how do I help you? How do I help get you clean?"

"Anchorette, I have to go through what is called detox, cold turkey. It's going to be hard, but once I have gone through that bit then I need to avoid the typical temptations. Once counsellors see that I'm trying they should help me, but I can't do this alone. You are the only other person who can help me, please." Aine was shaking.

Anchorette was her last hope of getting drug-free for good. "Look, I'm not saying no, okay, but I have to think about this and I have Joe to consider in all this." Aine made a face at Joe's name. "He is my husband, you know, and I also have Keith in this as well," Anchorette said firmly.

"Keith?" Aine asked.

"Yes, Keith, your nephew. I'm a mum as well as a worker," Anchorette said, a little calmer.

"I'm an aunt? I have a nephew, wow, I didn't know that," Aine said, surprised.

Anchorette waited a second or so for the news to sink in and then realized she had to get to work.

"Listen, I have to get into work now, as it is I'm running late. I finish in twelve hours' time. Can you come back here at eight? I will take you home. I don't know what or how I'm going to explain this one to Joe, but you're my sister and you're right, you do need help. Some way or another you need it."

Aine looked up at her. "You have a son who needs you more than I. I don't have any right to take his mother's time away from him. I should go."

Aine started to get up. Anchorette helped her but held her arm firmly and said, "Oh no, you don't! You promise me that you will be back here when my shift has finished. Promise me! I need you, and so do our mum and dad and now your nephew, too. Please promise me," Anchorette said, looking right into Aine's eyes. Standing there still gripping Aine's arm, she knew one thing about Aine: when she made a promise she always came good. Anchorette remembered that the time she was being bullied by Frankie and Freddie Gemmerson at school, Aine snuck into the boys' locker room and shredded their uniforms into pieces and flushed their trainers down the toilet. Aine had promised the two boys that if they didn't leave Anchorette alone she would get her revenge. Aine hadn't let Anchorette down then, so all she had to do was get her to promise.

"Promise me," Anchorette said, holding Aine's arm and waiting for a reply.

"Okay, I will be here, I promise. You go off to work—I will be here when you're finished."

Aine smiled. Anchorette let go of her arm to put both arms around her. As they hugged, Anchorette wrinkled her nose. "You're going for a hot bath, that's for sure, and I'm burning your clothes. My washing machine would just die if I tried to wash them and I can't afford a new one. Plus, I just figured out how to work the bloody thing!" They both laughed. As Anchorette walked up the drive away from Aine, she kept turning around, hoping that she was still the Aine who kept her promises and didn't break them. Anchorette had to hope that she was, as all she had left now was hope.

Chapter Four

Aine

As Aine watched her sister walking up the drive to the nursing home, Anchorette turned around to see her still standing there. *Just a few more seconds*, she thought as Anchorette went indoors and out of sight. The front door closed, and Aine collapsed against the tree from exhaustion and tiredness.

She had walked from the city to the sleepy little town she had grown up in. She had hated growing up in a town where everyone knew her business. Even as child she was labelled a freak and people whispered things about her behind her back. As soon as she was old enough to start staying out and going to all-night parties to forget her days she was lost to her family.

Aine remembered that as a child, when she told her mother that she could see Grandmama Hartwood and her aunt Hettie, her mother told her she was lying. The doctors said that she would eventually grow out of the lies and that she was just finding it difficult to let go. But it wasn't just Grandmama or Hettie that she saw; in truth, she saw a lot of spirits talking to her, and she didn't understand as a young child that it was not normal to talk and have contact with them.

When she attended her first party the girls shunned her, knowing she was different. The boys viewed her as a challenge to see how easy she was, and while she didn't give herself away freely, she made sure they were so drunk that they would assume she had when they passed out. She would stumble back to her parents' house and climb into bed to brace herself for the morning lectures from her mother on how she would ruin her life if she continued to carry on in this way. In truth her life was already ruined, not understanding all that was happening to her. Her father just sat there in agreement with her mother's verbal bullying, nodding his head and rarely speaking. They doted more on Anchorette, as she was better behaved.

The alcohol only numbed her feelings for a short while, but drugs were more effective. She could remember the first time everything just went blank. It was like someone had switched off the signal and she was alone. It was comforting to silence the voices; they could no longer hum in her head and talk to her. She welcomed loneliness for her company, but though it was her only companion, it couldn't help her.

I need to get out of here and find a place to hide without being seen, she thought, still leaning against the tree. The bar on the outskirts of town had been closed for some time. It was one of the things about this town—it wouldn't modernize to keep up with the kids, so businesses closed down just as quickly as they opened. She decided to go there. On the way, she saw a milkman making his deliveries, and so she headed in the direction in which he had just come. The front steps of the first three houses were empty, but at the fourth were some milk and bread. It was a start. She moved quickly down the path. As soon as she had both items, she sped out into a jog around the corner and down an alley. A bubble of laughter crept out, and she realized she hadn't done that in years.

"You know that it is good to hear your laughter, but could you please try to laugh about something that is not about stealing, Aine?" Aine looked up to see her aunt Hettie staring down at her.

"This day is going to be a long one," Aine said as she opened the loaf of bread and stuffed it into her mouth. It was dry and so she opened the milk in a rush and spilled it down her chin.

"How attractive," Aunt Hettie said.

"Hey, I'm hungry and need to eat. God, I need a hit," Aine said, looking up. "I honestly don't know if I can do this, Aunt Hettie. What you're asking me to do is crazy, and it just doesn't make it easy with you and Grandmama popping in and out all the time. Also, you never told me that Anchorette already had a son. This is hardly fair. I know Joe is a creep but are you sure?" Aine asked, taking out another slice of bread and folding it in half, taking more time to eat it.

"If you were to stay in reality long enough you to would hear the rumours. There is danger coming our way, and we have to make a start now in protecting our families," Aunt Hettie answered. "If we don't, we are all lost to the evilness that seeks to kill our lives, yours included, Aine. You need to sober up and fast!" Aunt Hettie finished off before disappearing.

"So, no pressure then?" Aine said, finishing off the slice and getting up. She was alone in the alleyway, but she knew people would start to come out of their houses to get in their cars to drive off to work. She got up and headed towards the outskirts of town, where the building would provide her with some shelter and most likely the unwanted company of lingering spirits. "Great, just flippin' great," she mumbled to herself.

Chapter Five

Anchorette

Work flew by real quickly, too quickly. Anchorette forgot to take Mrs. Potts off the toilet, and twenty minutes later a work colleague asked her if she had forgotten anything on the third floor; as she went through the checklist in her head she was overtaken by horror and embarrassment. After she apologized to her coworker she went to apologize to an upset Mrs. Potts. She explained that her mind was defiantly fast asleep, and that earlier she had accidentally filled up the sugar pot with salt, causing Miss Levy to swallow a mouthful of salt with her tea. That put a smile on Mrs. Potts's face, as Miss Levy hated her cat, Mr. Darcy, and at every opportunity she would try to run Mr. Darcy over with her Zimmer frame. During Anchorette's break time, she confided in the matron about Aine and asked her how to get through this. The matron said that she would make inquiries for Anchorette and have some information for her at the end of her shift. She also commented on the article of clothing that was missing from her uniform, and that that should not happen again.

At lunchtime Anchorette received a phone call from her mother, who was calling to tell her that Aine had visited her that morning and that Anchorette should watch out for her trying to get money off of her. When Anchorette told her that Aine had already seen her that morning and she had not given her any money but intended to help her, Janet rudely pointed out that she should be putting Keith first and not her sister. Anchorette said she had had enough and that maybe Janet should take her own advice and look after both her daughters. She hung up abruptly, knowing that she would have to apologize to her. Could her day get any worse?

In short, yes. Mr. Finnley dropped dead at teatime with his face straight into his bowl—death by drowning in asparagus and leek soup, of course. Who knew that asparagus was that much of an aphrodisiac to get the heart racing into a heart attack? It upset all the other residents, and they lost their appetites. Anchorette couldn't blame them; she didn't feel up to eating either after they removed Mr. Finnley's body to his room for to be cleaned and readied for the undertakers.

Finally work was finished. Anchorette quickly went to see the matron, who handed her a list of numbers to call on Monday morning for help. Anchorette then quickly raced down to the end of the drive. She could not see Aine, and her heart sank a little. Maybe she was running a little late. When Anchorette got to the corner of the drive, she stood and waited but did not have to wait long. She heard a muffled sound and then a thud. She turned around to see that Aine had been in the tree behind her. She smiled and hugged Aine.

"Did you think that I would not keep my promise to my sister?" Aine asked.

"I couldn't see you—I thought you might be running late, as I didn't know if you had a watch on you or not and, well, I don't know. Aine, you're my sister. It has been four years and we have both changed a lot. I'm just glad that you have not changed there."

Aine looked at Anchorette and then said, "Yes, we have both changed, one more so than the other. I cannot believe that you're a mother. You will have to tell me all about it, but firstly I think we should make a move, as one, it is still raining, and two, I don't want to hang around on street corners. A police car drove past four times on this road in the last ten minutes, and that was the reason I was up a tree. You know how bad it looks when someone like me is hanging around on a street corner." She smiled and chuckled a little. They linked arms and started walking home.

Anchorette couldn't help but wonder what sort of a person her sister had become, and what had driven her to think it was a good idea to hide up a tree. But instead of asking her, she figured she would tackle that one at a later date.

It was not uncomfortable walking her back to the house, but Anchorette's stomach began to tighten at the thought of how Joe would react. The sisters talked about Keith and the cats and how far Anchorette had come in life and the achievements she had made in her weekend job. It was small talk but it was nice, and Aine listened quite intently. They both were quiet for the rest of the ten-minute journey, Aine clearly not wanting to speak about her last four years, and then they were there at the front door.

"You sure you want to do this? I mean, it's not like I'm not grateful for what you're doing for me, it's just that I know Joe is going to be really mad with you for bringing me into your home. It's not like we have the greatest in-law relationship, and I know that is partly due to me always being a cow around him." Aine looked at Anchorette, waiting for an answer, but she could not back out now. Now was not the time to be weak. She had to take the next step and be strong for the both of them. This was her sister—it had to be now, or this chance might never come around again.

Anchorette swallowed deeply. "I'm sure you need help. You're my sister, and I have as much right to have you here as he has to any family who needs help in bad times. Besides, it's me who will be here for you. He will be at work, and I'll be taking the next month or so off to help you get through this. I cleared it with the matron today and she understands. She has also given me a phone number to call on Monday morning for advice on what I should be doing. Everything will be fine." Anchorette smiled, held her hand, and opened the front door.

The lights were on and she knew by the look on Joe's face that he knew. Janet must have already told him, because he looked mad. Anchorette turned to Aine and said, "Aine, go upstairs and run yourself a bath. The towels are in the cupboard next to the bathroom door. Just go up straight ahead, okay?" Anchorette smiled at her again and motioned for her to go up the stairs. Aine did so with her head down. Anchorette and Aine both knew that Joe was going to say things that Aine was in no fit state to hear, and that it would not be pleasant at all.

"What the hell are you playing at? I thought you knew not to ever bring her here, ever. She is the lowest of the low. She is scum, and you brought scum into this house and into your son's life. You know how dangerous she is. I'm surprised that the police didn't pick her up outside your work." Joe added that last bit with smugness in his voice, but also realized he had slipped up.

The knotted tension in Anchorette's stomach was pulling tighter, and she took in a raspy breath. It hurt Anchorette to know that he was enjoying what he was doing. She looked at him with tears beginning to swell in her eyes, not wanting to cry. "You called the police on her? She needs help, not a few nights in the cell. She wants to get clean. She has been living on the streets for the past couple weeks. This is my sister, and she is as much my family as you and Keith are. Mum and Dad have turned their backs on her. I'm all she has left, and I told her that I would be there for her. I can't throw her out, she needs help. Please, just let her have a bath, some food, and a night's sleep here, and then in the morning we can all sit down and discuss this rationally, please?" Joe saw the hurt in Anchorette's eyes and did not like it one bit. Maybe because he thought he had caused it, but then he realized she had to work the next day and snapped at her, "You have work tomorrow, and I'm not babysitting her!"

Anchorette was not looking forward to confronting this next bit so soon, but as they were at that bridge she said calmly but firmly, "I have taken a couple weeks off so that I can be there for her." Joe's face went from red to purple. He stormed into the kitchen, grabbed his car keys, and then headed to the back door. He didn't say anything else, he was too mad. He slammed the back door without giving a backward glance and headed down into the back garden. Anchorette heard the car door slam and the engine rev before he took off. She knew where he would be heading: to the snooker club. His mate Martin would be there, and he would probably stay at his house. She knew that he would not want to be in the house that night or in the morning, and she didn't want him there anyway. Not after he told her about the police. That hurt just a little too deeply.

Chapter Six

Joe

After Joe slammed the back door he saw the neighbour on the right conveniently pottering about in the garden. *More like she had heard raised voices and had raced to hear the gossip,* he thought. He turned and looked her squarely in the eyes. *I want to rip a head clean off, but I wasn't trained to hurt innocent humans, be they nosey or not.* She looked away and jogged as fast as her fat little legs would carry her back into her house. He turned to the back gate and took a little frustration out on the hinges.

How I hate this whole life I am leading. I just want to abandon it all, but I can't with Aine being here. She is a loose cannon that could potentially explode and rip everything apart. Exiting the alleyway he unlocked the car door with the remote on his keychain. He got in the car and could see a shadow in the upstairs bathroom window.

It would have been so easy to grab the gun. But if I took her out now I would obviously be the main suspect. No, I have to think this one through. I have to make a strategy and a good one and follow it to the end.

The engine revved as he switched it on. He put it into first gear and punched the accelerator with his foot, knowing where he was going to go. *Anchorette will assume I am going to Martin's, and if I were any half-decent married man, I would, perhaps.* But he didn't head west. Instead he headed north, out of the town where his life was suffocated on regular basis due to a loveless marriage. *I hate being to married a woman I can't and don't love. But I also hate myself for treating her this way.*

Anchorette had no idea as to what she was and the potential she had. He had been assigned—no, ordered—many years ago to marry her by the company that he worked for. It was all a ruse to get her pregnant and to train their kids to become skilled to take out her sort. He was given orders to give her tonics to encourage her to become pregnant.

There was nothing he could do about it. He had been conceived in a similar way. His birth mother, whom he couldn't even remember, was told he had died in childbirth. His father knew differently, as he had visited his newborn son daily, along with some of his other children who had "died in childbirth." There were times he wanted to so desperately see his mother and he knew where she lived, but he also knew that he would be found out. Anchorette's mother, Janet, was the closest he could ever get to having a mother figure, and she made his skin crawl every time. *I just can't understand how she could treat her children and husband the way she did,* he thought about his mother. *It must have been the money. She was always so eager to climb the ladder of society and show off.*

His breathing became a little more relaxed, and he dialled the number to Martin's. It rang but there was no reply, so he left a message on the answering machine to let him know that Anchorette might call. Then he rang a second number.

"Hello?" answered a sleepy voice.

"It's me. Let me in, I'm around the corner." The phone line died and he turned the corner to park. It was a busy street and parking was difficult but he found a space. He turned the engine off and looked up to a block of flats. On the balcony he could see her in a red silk gown, smiling down at him. *She has always known that she is the only woman I have ever needed. I so desperately need her right now.*

He got out of the car, locked it up, and went to the entrance and into the lobby. His heart was pounding hard and he could feel the blood numb all the anger out of him. The lift doors opened and he stepped in. Fortunately she was only three levels up, and when the doors opened she was standing there at the door to her flat with two drinks in her hands. He raised an eyebrow at her, stepped towards her, took the drink in one hand, and grabbed her with the other hand. His lips crushed down on hers hard and hungry as he pushed her back into the flat and kicked the front door shut.

Chapter Seven

Anchorette

Anchorette had known that Aine was going to present a problem, but she hadn't imagined it would be this bad. Anchorette turned to go up the stairs, wiping the tear that had fallen down her cheek and trying to calm herself down before seeing Aine.

Aine was sitting on the toilet seat with the lid down as Anchorette entered. The bath water was nearly high enough, and the heavy smell of bergamot oil lingered in the air.

"He called the police on me, didn't he," Aine said. It was not a question.

"You heard?" Anchorette asked.

Aine nodded. "I think I should leave in the morning and stay out of your life for good. He sounded really mad with you and he has not even spoken to me yet, so I can only imagine how much venom he has in store for me. Plus, he is right—I am scum, and that's not good for you or Keith!"

Aine looked washed-out and there was no way that Anchorette was going to allow anything else to happen to her. She looked at her straight in the face and said, "Take a bath. There will be clean pyjamas out by the door. I'm going downstairs to get us both some food. And you are not scum—you are my sister, and if you're scum, well, then you'd better clean up your act because I'm not wasting my time."

Before Aine could say anything, Anchorette turned and walked out, closing the door behind her, and then went to get some pyjamas for Aine. Aine would have to hold up the bottoms, though, as she had lost so much weight with the drugs that she had taken, and with Anchorette still having extra weight after having Keith, and so she decided to get a couple safety pins. Anchorette left them outside the bathroom door and went to the kitchen to see what she could cook in twenty minutes or less. Anchorette was not in the mood for anything too complicated. By the time she had finished putting the last touches on a couple BLTs, Aine had come down the stairs trying very hard not to laugh at the pins holding her bottoms up.

"You know what, if you bent over, there would be a full moon in Japan," said Aine. Anchorette just looked at her, and though she thought it was cruel, she took it.

"You know what, if you lose any more weight, you will fall through your knickers and end up hanging yourself. Now here, have a sandwich before I decide to block out Australia too." They both burst into laughter.

"Anchorette, you have definitely changed. You would have cried a few years ago if I had said that to you. Who are you, and what have you done with the real Anchorette?" Aine said, laughing and taking a bite of her sandwich.

"It's called daytime TV and being pregnant. Joe doesn't like it when I say those sorts of comments, but at work I usually hear it anyway from staff and so I just picked it up," she said while shrugging her shoulders and taking a big bite. It was too hot, but it felt good to get food into her.

"Okay, so you're telling me that you are the dutiful wife to Joe and you're little miss prim and proper around him, and yet at work you're someone else altogether? I thought I had problems with my personality, but you take that one," she said, laughing again.

"It's not easy with Joe to speak my mind so freely. You know, that's one of the reasons he does not like you very much," Anchorette said, smiling.

"Hey, I thought it was just my five finger discount and addiction he didn't like. I had no idea he hated my charming and sparkling personality too, but I will keep that one in mind for the meeting tomorrow at breakfast. That is, of course, as long as I make it through the night without being thrown out by him," Aine said, taking another bite of the sandwich.

"Oh, you can sleep safely, don't worry. He will be out all night. He had that look of 'don't wait up for me I'm staying out all night, and I won't be there for the morning chat either,'" Anchorette said.

Aine looked at her, swallowed her mouthful, and then said, "I haven't been here for a day and I have already driven you and Joe to have an argument, and him to sleep somewhere else tonight. He really is not going to want you to help me, and I don't want to put a strain on your marriage. Maybe I should just leave tomorrow."

Anchorette shuffled from one foot to the other. She didn't like having arguments with Joe, either, but she had to do something. Anchorette looked at Aine and said, "Hey, if you're just looking for an excuse to carry on with your addiction, then use something else, because Joe is the really sad one. If you have not got the strength and want to give up, then say so. I will go down to the bank tomorrow and withdraw a couple hundred. That would be enough to get you through for a day or so? Nothing like proving Joe that he's right and I'm wrong." Aine looked hurt that Anchorette could have said something like that. "All I'm trying to say is that I'm in it from the start to the end, but you have to be, too. I can only help and hold your hand—I can't actually do this for you .You know that, so how about we put Joe out of the picture? He is my problem, not yours."

Aine came across to the other side of the kitchen counter to give Anchorette a hug and whispered, "I'm in if you are." At that point Anchorette didn't know exactly just how relevant those five words would be. It was then that she noticed that Aine had lost control of her balance and had slumped herself against Anchorette and the kitchen counter. She was quite cold but sweating, which Anchorette hadn't noticed before. "Guess I should get to my bed and stay there for a while—the withdrawal has started to kick in. I have not used for a day and a bit now." She gave Anchorette a halfhearted glance and smiled. Anchorette looked at her and nodded, afraid at this point that if she said anything her voice might crack and then she would be of no use. Anchorette took most of Aine's body weight—not that there was much to take, what with her being so tiny—but they managed to get up the stairs. Once at the top Aine lurched forward. At first Anchorette couldn't quite make out what exactly she was doing, but then it started: a night of Aine vomiting into the basin.

Anchorette ended up sleeping in the chair that she had used when breastfeeding Keith. She hardly got much sleep, for just as she thought that Aine was finished being sick and was getting to the subconscious stage of sleep, it would happen again. At about 4.30 a.m. Aine also had diarrhoea, and Anchorette was concerned that she would become dehydrated. Finally she drifted off to sleep just a couple hours before Keith would wake up and a few hours before Joe would be home. *How am I ever supposed to sleep with the Joe situation still to come?* she thought, but surprisingly she drifted off.

Anchorette awoke at 7.00 a.m. to Keith's cries; he was at the teething stage. She knew she had to help Aine, but her timing sucked. But would there ever be a good time for Anchorette to support Aine? She knew Joe's answer to this one—NEVER—and could even imagine him saying the word to her face. So now had to be the time. It still sucked, though.

Chapter Eight

Anchorette

Anchorette got up to get Keith out of his cot bed, but he was not in his room. She heard his cries again, but they were coming from her bedroom. She walked quietly across the creaky floorboards to peek around the bedroom door. There on the bed was Joe cradling Keith in his arms, trying to soothe him with his teething blanket. Keith was not having it. Anchorette caught Keith's attention, which led Joe to look at her, too.

He looked calm and his eyes held no hint of anger. "Morning. You look tired. Do you want me to take Keith for the day? You look like you could do with a few more hours of sleep."

Could she be hearing right? Was she still sleeping? Was Joe really being that nice to her? "You're not still mad at me?" she asked him in a whisper.

"I'm frustrated as hell that you excluded me from the choice to look after Aine. It would have been nice if you had spoken to me about it first, but I do understand. It's not like my heart is made of stone," he said with a little lightness. "She is your sister, a bond that can't be broken even after what has happened in the past. Come here and sit next to us." He held out his hand to her. Anchorette moved slowly over to them both. She was still tired but figured she may as well as throw herself into the conversation while he was in a reasonable mood. Who knew when this might happen again?

Keith was now playing peek-a-boo with his blanket and had somewhat stopped his grizzly noisemaking. "Okay, so let's talk about what we can do to help Aine, then," said Joe. He gave her a look that suggested that it was not going to be an easy compromise of any sort, but that he was willing to hear it.

Anchorette started off by admitting her mistake. "Yes, you are right. I was wrong to not have discussed it with you first, but I was kind of caught off-guard. I saw her just before I went to work yesterday, and then at work mother called and was nasty to me. I was already having a bad morning, and to be honest it was a bad afternoon, too. One of the patients died, and I had to get Aine to promise to meet me after work. She might have left town otherwise, and she was pleading—no, begging—for my help after Mum had turned her away. I can't turn her away. If it was Keith with an addiction, would you or could you turn him away? I'm so sorry, Joe. Please understand that I have no intention to hurt you." She was so tired that her tears caught her a little off-guard, but she also hoped that it would soften Joe up just a little. She knew that it was a slight weak point for him to see her cry.

Joe took a deep breath and composed himself before speaking. Anchorette could tell that this could go either way with him, and she was hoping that it would go her way. "You help get her clean, and then she moves out. That is it—nothing more, nothing less. You know that if it was Keith that I would never turn my back on him, but Keith is my son, and this is why I'm also saying this. Aine gets clean and then she is out—I mean it. You're a mother to our son, not to your sister, and while I don't agree with your choice to help her, I can see and understand why. Just don't expect me to like it. You know that I find her rude and bad-mannered, and those are just the qualities at the surface of her personality. I don't want whatever else is there to have an effect on Keith, okay? I know that you are sorry, too, and I'm sorry for taking off like that last night. I had a day of your mother and I don't need to tell you what that was like." While supporting Keith with one hand he put his arm around Anchorette and kissed her forehead. "I love you, Anchorette, but please don't let her drive a wedge between us."

Anchorette looked up at him. She could not understand where all the understanding was coming from, but she was glad that all of her hoping had paid off. She looked up at him and said, "I love you, too. I love both of my men, you and Keith, and as soon as Aine is well enough I will help her to move to a flat or clinic. I just have to make sure that she is really okay. I don't want to fail where Mum and Dad have, okay?"

Joe got up with Keith and headed towards the door. "Just get some sleep, you look real tired," he said, and with that he went downstairs with Keith.

Anchorette returned to the room Aine was in and fell asleep in the rocking chair.

Chapter Nine

Anchorette

Anchorette got another hour or so of sleep before Aine woke up shaking. Sweat was dripping off her. Anchorette got up from her nursing chair and went to grab a flannel from the cupboard in the bathroom. She ran it under the cold tap and washed down Aine's face, neck, and hands. Anchorette then went back into her bedroom to find the number to the help centre that the matron had given her the night before. She found her mobile phone in her jacket pocket, which was slung across the chair at her dresser table, and dialled it even though it was Sunday. She hoped that if she got an answering service, they would not take too long to get back to her. Anchorette felt useless at not being able to do much to help Aine, but dialling the number at least was something. The answering machine beeped and told her to leave a message if it was of importance, so she explained about Aine going through detox.

After she hung up she spent the rest of the morning keeping Aine's fluid intake up as much as possible, holding her hair back when most of it came up again, and helping her to the toilet. That was the worst of all, as Aine had little control of herself. Anchorette was grateful when she received a phone call that afternoon from a Dr. Jade.

He was very helpful in reassuring Anchorette that she was doing the right thing in just keeping her fluids up. He was a realist and told her that Aine should come to his clinic as soon as possible, but with Aine in pain and refusing to go, it was hard. The doctor told Anchorette it would be in her best interest, and while she more than agreed with him, he also told her it was Aine's choice and that she could leave at any time if she really didn't want to stay.

Anchorette knew that Aine had been locked up in a clinic in the past and it had never worked out, but this time was different: it was with her.

The doctor heard Aine in the background telling Anchorette what she thought about going into a clinic, and he gave Anchorette as much advice as he could. Although she knew the doctor had heard it, she could not help but smile. Aine was determined to have her own way.

Dr. Jade explained that stays lasted on average for about five to seven days, ten at the most. The symptoms would be flu-like: vomiting and diarrhoea. Anchorette was mentally ticking off all he was saying and mentally gearing up for a week's worth of it.

Towards the end of the call Dr. Jade tried to persuade Anchorette to bring Aine in Monday morning to assess her, but Aine told the doctor to take his clinic and shove it up his ass. "Pleasant, isn't she?" was all Anchorette could think of to say. She could not help but wonder if a bad temper was also a symptom.

Anchorette hung up and walked back into the room Aine was staying in and gave her a stern look. "That was very rude of you to have said that, you know," she said while wiping down Aine's face and hands again.

Aine looked at Anchorette. "We made a deal, you know, and I don't need a clinic to tell me how to do this. It doesn't work for me, Anchorette. We both know that."

She had a point, and at least Anchorette could keep an eye on her while she was there.

Aine took a few more sips of water and, as gently as she could, moved to her side and lay down. Anchorette sat in the chair and waited to see if she was going to be sick again, but she was not and eventually drifted off to sleep.

At this point Anchorette took the opportunity to go downstairs with the dirty laundry and put on a washing load. She could hear the TV: Joe was watching sport with Keith, and she guessed it was a bloke-bonding thing. She didn't know what Joe would have done if it had been a girl. Maybe he would have locked her in an ivory tower, never to date a man ever? Or maybe he would have encouraged her to be a tomboy, into sports and scraped kneecaps and playing football with the boys? Either way it was not something she had to worry about: Keith was only still a baby, and it was too soon to be thinking about baby number two, mentally, physically, financially, or any other -ally!

Anchorette went in the lounge and sat next to Joe. He leant over and kissed her, still in a good mood. Well, she wasn't knocking it.

"What's the time?" Anchorette asked, looking to find the remote control to get the clock up on the TV.

"It's just after three. Keith and I have been out to the park this morning, but it started to get a little cloudy and there was a light shower of rain, so we came back, had some lunch, and then both decided to watch sport this afternoon after he had a nap for a couple hours."

There were some days when he just took Anchorette's breath away, and this was one of them. "I love you so much that I could marry you, if you were not already married to a lucky woman," she said.

Joe looked at her and leant over to whisper in her ear, "You're all the luck I ever need—that's why I married you," and then he leant over even further to kiss her neck and throat.

Keith let out a giggle at what he was seeing. It brought them back to reality, which was just as well, as Anchorette was hungry and needed food. Anchorette got up, and as she headed to the kitchen she turned to ask if Joe or Keith needed anything from the kitchen. They were both good and set for the football, so it was just herself who needed food. Anchorette decided that after she had eaten a bowl of cereal she would check up on Aine to see if she could at least get some more water into her, as the last thing Anchorette wanted to do was let her dehydrate on top of everything else. On the way upstairs Anchorette thought it would be a good time to freshen up and get into some clean pyjamas, as she smelled bad after yesterday's work and also with Aine's throwing up: she could smell it in the air as she walked passed Aine's room and into her bedroom again. Once clean Anchorette took a few calming breaths on her way to Aine's room. Aine's hair was sticking out in tufts under the duvet, and she was snoring lightly.

Anchorette turned to look as the door moved slightly. Minstral padded in, wondering what was happening; he looked up at Anchorette and meowed and purred. He wandered over to the nursing chair, jumped up, and circled a few times on the blanket, kneading it with his claws before realizing that it was not a good idea. Stuck, he tried his best to free his paw from the wool blanket. Anchorette chuckled at how daft the cat could be.

He looked at her, tilted his head to one side, and meowed, his tail whipping as if telling her it was stupid of her to have put a woollen blanket on the chair in the first place! He then curled up and purred just loudly enough to cause Aine to snore more deeply. With that Anchorette leaned over the nursing chair and scratched him between the ears before walking out the room and down to the garage to get the air bed.

Anchorette had decided her back was not up to the task of sleeping in the nursing chair, and given that Minstral had just taken up post there, she may as well get the flippin' thing blown up and ready for the next week or so. She grabbed the air bed from the garage, and when she opened the door that led from the garage to the kitchen to go back inside, she found Joe standing there.

He saw the blow-up bed and sighed heavily. He didn't like the thought of her spending time away from him at night, and she could feel a little tension.

Was he going to be that difficult after being so understanding just an hour or so ago? Anchorette didn't know, but she took the air bed upstairs into Keith's bedroom to start pumping it up. The air bed could be carried into Aine's room in a little while, and she'd check up on her and get some more fluid into her.

"Aine, time to wake up. Come on, just for a little while— just so that I can get some water into you." Minstral was still there and gave Anchorette a little meow, and then got up, stretched, and walked towards the end of the nursing chair. He was not the only one stretching. Aine too had started to stir, but her calm peacefulness was broken by a gurgling sound, and she lurched headfirst towards the basin to throw up again. After she had finished and Anchorette had cleaned out the basin, Anchorette left the room to get a small glass of water and a clean flannel to wash Aine's face and hands.

"Feeling better?" Anchorette asked as she went back into the room and gave Aine the flannel. Aine took it, and then Anchorette opened the window to let in some air. She needed to get rid of the smell until she had the opportunity to go to the shop and get some carpet cleaning product.

"I must look and smell really bad, huh?" Aine said guiltily.

"Well, I wasn't expecting this to be easy, but you know, I'm wondering how much more vomit you are going to produce. I think you broke the world record last night, so any time you want to stop is okay by me," Anchorette said, trying to be okay about it, but to be honest it was not okay. Still, she had to be there, as Aine needed her.

"Yeah, sorry about that. I guess it can't get any worse with the throwing up, at least. But my stomach is hurting so much, and my body is aching, too."

As Aine said this, Anchorette handed her the glass of water and Aine looked up at her. Anchorette wished she could do something to take the pain and hurt away, but she knew that Aine had to feel the pain. If she was to ever have any hope of staying clean, she needed to remember this part as well. Dr. Jade had mentioned methadone, but this was going to be a tricky subject.

Anchorette sucked in a deep breath and said, "Well, I can't do much for the pain. But Dr. Jade did say that if you wanted to go and get checked out medically, he could also prescribe you some medication so that you are not suffering as much." Aine scowled at Anchorette, so Anchorette continued in a lighter, more encouraging voice. "But here is some water. I think if you take small sips then it might just stay down. After that we should at least get you into the bathroom if you need to go to the toilet."

Aine took the water and drank a small mouthful. "Ugh, that tastes gross. I think I might have to use some toothpaste while I'm in the bathroom, too. I might be in pain and smell nasty, but I would like to at least try to enjoy some water without the aftertaste."

The women looked at each other. It was tense and awkward, but then Anchorette sat beside Aine and said, "I know this is difficult for you, but please don't let me down, okay? I couldn't go through all this again."

Aine looked at her and then said, "I don't want to go through this again, either, and I promise that I won't let you down." And with that a tear fell and a smile broke across Anchorette's face. That was all she needed to hear.

They headed towards the bathroom to tidy Aine up just a little. Aine was grateful for the minty taste of toothpaste, and Anchorette's nose was grateful, too. Aine took her time walking back to the bed; she told Anchorette it felt like pins and needles were stabbing her body everywhere. Aine sat up in bed and then Minstral walked back in through the window; once in the room he jumped up onto the bed and meowed at Aine.

"Who is this, then?" Aine asked while Minstral got closer to her and gently nudged her hand.

"This is Minstral. I have another two cats, both female. Minstral is the only male cat. He was watching you while I was downstairs talking to Joe," Anchorette explained.

"How is Joe? Has he calmed down yet, or should I be prepared to hear you two yelling some more?" Aine asked while Minstral nudged a little more, asking to be scratched behind an ear.

"He has calmed down, but he does not want you here any longer than is necessary. He feels that you are a bad influence on Keith—he is just being an overprotective father. So I told him that once you are all better I will help you find a place and help you move in, and then I'll help you get a job—if you want me to, that is. I don't want to overstep the mark as to what your plans are," Anchorette said with a hopeful smile.

Aine smiled back and said, "One step at a time. Next you will be matching me up and planning my wed—" But before Aine could finish her sentence, she grabbed for the basin again. It seemed that little and often was not the way to go regarding drinking water.

Anchorette took the basin once Aine was finished to clean it out. When Anchorette came back into the bedroom, Aine was already drifting off to sleep with Minstral purring next to her. Guessing that everything had been taking its toll on her mentally and physically, Anchorette left her to sleep, going back downstairs to Joe and Keith.

The football had already started, so she just sat next to them, but about an hour or so later Anchorette decided that she should crack on with the laundry and dinner. She was not too sure what Joe wanted to eat and she hated to disturb him in his football match, but food had to be dealt with at some point.

"Hon, what do you want to eat tonight?" Anchorette asked, trying not to distract him too much.

He looked at her and said, "You're taking the night off. I thought we would get takeaway tonight, what with you being tired and stuff. I don't want to replace the kitchen because you fell asleep at the cooker," he said with a grin.

Anchorette was confused. In all their married days, not once had they ever ordered takeaway. All this niceness was starting to ring a large alarm bell, but she smiled at him and said, "Okay, hon, what do you want to order?" Although Anchorette was grateful that he was being so understanding, she had a feeling that a lot of understanding would be required. Something that was not Joe's strongest point.

Chapter Ten

Anchorette

Days and nights rolled together for the next ten days. Aine was still throwing up food—even soup and water was hit-or-miss. Anchorette had phoned Dr. Jade to ask him about it, and he said that it was to be expected and it would pass. He also told Anchorette that getting clean was not the hardest part—it was staying clean and avoiding temptations that would be most difficult for Aine. Anchorette didn't tell Aine that bit, as she had a feeling that Aine already knew that deep down, and it was the pain that she had not been so prepared for. But then again, Anchorette didn't know anyone who was.

They sat up one evening talking about Aine's boyfriend who had died, Brett Hunter. They had both known him at school. He was in a couple of Anchorette's classes: he had always been so quiet, a bit of a loner and a geek, and though he was intelligent he never had any friends. His older brother Dean had been intimidating: he was the popular one in that year, and one would never guess they were related. But Aine told Anchorette that Brett had completely changed his personality. He had reinvented himself: he had muscles and would have looked like a runway model if it weren't for his mohawk. Aine showed Anchorette a photo of the two of them together. Anchorette could tell that Aine was extremely sad to have lost him. Aine told her that it had been like losing her other half, and that she would never gain it back.

"It's like coffee without cream. It's okay to drink it black, but it won't taste as good if you don't have the cream. That's what my life will be like from now on. I can't change any of it, no matter how much I try." Anchorette could see that Aine had an interesting way of putting things and summing up her life at times.

They sat and talked for many hours about what Aine had been doing since they had last seen each other. Surprisingly, it was not all just sitting around and getting high all day, as Anchorette had thought it would be. Aine and Brett both went travelling. They had travelled to India, parts of Africa, Italy, and France. Aine especially loved France, not for the sightseeing, but for the food. Only in France would you order a horse hamburger or pig's trotters in a puff pastry with a creamy sauce and a bed of rice. Of course the frogs' legs and *escargot* had to be done. Anchorette envisioned Aine trying to crack open the shell like Julia Roberts in *Pretty Woman*, which they had watched when they were younger. They always swore that they would never be outwitted by a snail and his shell. It turned out that it was not at all difficult—it was all in the wrist action.

Anchorette felt a pang of jealousy at the experiences she'd had. With her bills and mortgage, a holiday was the last thing on a very long list. Maybe next year, but Anchorette doubted Joe would do France. It had been a push to get Joe to go to Italy on their honeymoon, and it ended up coinciding with football. Of course they made a compromise: he went to football, and Anchorette took a couple hours for pampering and shopping. England lost, but she made up for it that night. She had bought some sexy underwear, which she did not wear for long: once Joe saw it on her, he ripped it off. She was glad she had not told him how much he had ripped off, until the next morning, when Joe saw the receipt. There was no more alone time with his credit card after that.

Chapter Eleven

Anchorette

Aine was out of her bed two weeks after she arrived. Anchorette was glad of it. She had been doing overtime with laundry. Plus, with Joe at work, Anchorette had Keith to handle as well. By the eighth day, Aine had stopped vomiting and was starting to keep liquid and light food down. But Aine needed to build up her strength before any other plans could be put into action. When Aine did eventually start to venture out of her room, Anchorette was grateful for her company. During the day, some adult conversation was always welcome.

Janet called one morning, putting Anchorette in a bad mood. Janet told Anchorette in her authoritative voice that she was a fool to let Aine back into their lives, and that as soon as Anchorette cut all ties with Aine and came to her senses, then Janet would be prepared to allow Keith and Anchorette back into her life. Anchorette hated being left with ultimatums from anyone, but it would not have bothered her so much if it had come from anyone else. It really hurt to come from her mum, and it hurt that she would not hear of how well Aine was doing. Well, if Janet wanted to be stubborn, then so could Anchorette.

Aine knew that something was wrong by the way Anchorette was taking her frustration out on vacuuming, but she thought it was best to wait till she had finished attacking the skirting boards before asking her what was the matter. Then Aine saw Anchorette in the kitchen making up lunch with a knife in her hand, and she said jokingly, "Don't do it. How would I explain it to Joe? I would be the one getting the blame."

Anchorette looked up at her with a confused expression on her face. "What?" Anchorette asked, not really following what Aine had said in the first place.

"You have been spring cleaning so hard that the Hoover will need first aid. Plus, your face looks like it has done a few rounds with a wasp in your mouth, so either you're mad with me and about to let rip or you're mad with Joe, but I can't see it being Joe, as it was quiet this morning and I didn't hear anything being smashed. It must be me, as Keith is way too young to have done anything wrong, so spill. What have I done or not done?"

At this point Anchorette took a few breaths before saying the one simple word that would get the blood of both of them boiling: "Mother!" Anchorette heard the sharp intake of Aine's breath, which was followed by a long blowing-out noise.

"Okay, not quite what I was expecting just yet, but I knew the bridge was coming soon. So what was said, then?" Aine's reaction was not what Anchorette had expected; plus, she didn't want this to set her back.

The doorbell rang just as Anchorette was about to answer. She was glad that it would give her time to think about how to word her response now that she knew Aine's reaction was calm. Anchorette walked to the door and looked through the keyhole; she saw a bright yellow t-shirt and knew instantly who it was. Aine had followed Anchorette, and when she turned to face Aine, Aine mouthed the word *who?* Anchorette mouthed *Father* back to her. "Okay, let's get this over with," Aine said.

Anchorette opened the front door. There stood David wearing his bright t-shirt, black jeans, and a pair of Jesus sandals with thick woollen socks.

"Hey there, Dad, nice outfit. Where's the queen bee? Or have you left her in the car?" Aine said, trying to be upbeat and at the ready to defend herself should he start.

"Anchorette, your mother has sent me over here with Keith's belongings, as she feels that until you come to your senses we should stay out of each other's lives," David said, completely ignoring Aine's comment as well as her altogether.

"Wait, hold up, you are cutting Anchorette out of your lives along with Keith because of me?" The question was a mixture of shock, confusion, and disgust.

"That's what I was going to tell you about before the door went," Anchorette said, looking at her and thinking that this might send her over the edge. "But I will not be dictated to by Mother. Just because you two have made your choice does not mean that I have to make the same, seeing as I don't live under your roof any longer. Aine is welcome here for as long she needs me, and she has my full support," Anchorette said to David, waiting for him to explode.

"Where would you like Keith's items?" David asked. Anchorette could tell that he was determined not to get into an argument with either of them, as he would feel that lowering himself to this level was completely beneath him. What a wonderful role model!

"Well, I have no intention of seeing sense, so maybe you should donate to a charity shop. It was you and mother who bought those items, not me, and I most certainly do not need reminders of ultimatums around the house," Anchorette said. Two could play at this game, and Anchorette was not about to back down.

"Very well," David said, and turned to walk back to the car.

"Bet that put a sting in your plan," Aine said. She knew that their dad had heard it because his shoulders hunched a little, but he carried on walking to his car.

Anchorette closed the door and looked at Aine. They hugged. Anchorette was proud that Aine had handled the situation quite well. She was, however, was not looking forward to telling Joe about it tonight. *Maybe I should give him a call at work to give him a heads-up just in case Mother calls him?*

"Well, that was not awkward at all. I'm sorry that Mum and Dad are being so difficult. And you know that I'm okay, if you want to throw me out today so that you can rebuild what I have ruined," Aine said, looking concerned that Anchorette might just crumble into a heap to the ground. To be truthful, Anchorette wanted to, but she knew she had to stay strong. She could not allow her mother to dictate to her. Anchorette also knew that her mother would be stubborn and determined until she took her last breath, and even then might try from beyond the grave.

"No, it's okay, I have to take a stand at some point. If it was not about you, then it would be about Keith or Joe or something, and she would never give up till she got what she wanted. But for now I had better give Joe a call and let him know before she does," Anchorette said a little tiredly. She felt like the stuffing had been knocked out of her.

"Okay, so who are you and what have you done with my sister?" Aine asked, looking at Anchorette as though she was not quite sure if what she had just heard had actually come from her.

"I'm trying to make a stand, so a little support here would be nice," Anchorette said while heading for the phone.

"Okay, support is here. I owe you big time. I will leave you to make your call, and I will go check up on Keith see if he is awake."

Anchorette smiled at her, so proud at how far Aine had come. She gave her another hug.

Chapter Twelve

Anchorette

The secretary put Anchorette through to Joe, and after she told him what had happened, he went all quiet. After a long pause, he let out a long breath. She could tell that he was not happy about this.

"Can we discuss this when I get home?" he said. "I have a meeting in an hour's time with a client. I need to present a project to an American company who are only here for a few days. I really need to sell them this, or the company might start looking for someone else to take my place."

Anchorette thought that this might be the reason he had not been happy; maybe it hadn't been because of her. She knew the family feud was not going to get better anytime soon.

"Okay, Joe, sorry for disturbing you. It's just that I thought I would give you a heads-up just in case my mother did call you again. I didn't want to put you in that awkward situation. Good luck with this afternoon. Love you," she said, trying to sound positive for his meeting.

"Love you, too. But I don't know what time I will be home, as I don't know if I will have to go out to a meal with them or a few drinks. So you Keith and Aine should go ahead and eat without me tonight, okay?"

This was unlike Joe. Usually when he had meetings that ran beyond working hours, he would make it a point to come home as soon as he could to be with her and Keith. Again she tried to sound positive and not let what he had said bother her. "Okay, hon, I'll see you when I see you. Hope all goes well."

With that, Joe hung up. Anchorette knew that she should be happy that he was not mad at her and that he was trying to do his work well, but there was a thought niggling away in the back of her mind that not all really was well.

She decided to go upstairs and see how Aine and Keith were doing. Aine was standing in the doorway of Keith's bedroom. He was awake and making his gurgling sound. He was happy. Aine was looking at him in a wondering way.

Anchorette linked arms with Aine and said, "He looks happy now, but when that crappy nappy explodes, he looks the dead spit of Joe, you know." They both laughed.

"It's not that," Aine said. "It's just that I can't help but wonder, with the whole what-ifs, you know, if me and Brett would've had our own family someday. What sort of a family would we have been? Would we have been happy? How many kids would we have had?"

"Aine, Keith is coming up for seven months, and I can assure you that having baby number two is the very last thing on my mind, and not for financial reasons, either. It hurts like hell to push one of those out of a hole that is only ten centimetres dilated. As for what might have been, I know that Brett has recently died, but you cannot ever predict what is around the corner. Time will only tell. Even you could not have predicted at this time last year that you would now be standing here looking over your nephew. One day at a time, that's all that has to be done. With that in mind, how do you feel about us taking a walk to the local park this afternoon? Get us some air and an ice cream?"

Anchorette was trying to sell this idea to her, given that she had not set foot outside since arriving. Aine spent most of her time either in her bedroom or with Anchorette.

"I don't know if I'm quite ready for that. I know that you mean well, but could we leave it for a few more days? I still don't feel that all my strength is quite with me yet."

Anchorette looked at Aine. She knew that it was more than just the strength. It was also that she did not want to find temptation outside, and by staying indoors, what she could not see she could not find.

"Okay, but you know you will have to go out at some point. How about we make a date for next week for fifteen minutes in the car?" Anchorette thought that being in the car would be a chance to get out of the house without the temptation.

"Okay, I will try really hard, but I'm not making any promises, all right?"

"It's a start," Anchorette said with a smile.

"Hey, does Joe know about the other woman you're planning to meet up with next week to take out for a car ride? Is he going to get jealous?" Aine asked with laughter in her voice.

It felt good to Anchorette to hear her talk that way; it been a long time since they had last connected like this, so she decided to go with it. "What Joe does not know cannot hurt him, so I won't tell him if you don't. But just to be clear, you ain't floating my boat, sister or not." They both laughed hard, and even Keith joined in, which made them laugh even harder. Keith's laugh was a dirty laugh that was very infectious—when heard, it could not be resisted.

"You know," Aine said, "I hope I get a chance to be more in his life. He is such a beautiful boy. Even if he is half of Joe, he still has more of you in him."

That afternoon they spent playing in the lounge with Keith, watching the babies' TV channel and pretending to be characters from the shows. Anchorette did a very good Telletubby, while Aine did an excellent voice-over of Makka Pakka from *In the Night Garden*. It made Keith laugh and tired him out, and it also took Anchorette's mind off Joe and how he had been that morning, at least until Aine bought it up while she started cooking dinner. Anchorette was not sure what to say or how to word what she was thinking, but Aine got the gist of it.

"I'm obviously putting a strain on your relationship. Maybe I should move out and let you guys get back to normality and be a family unit again."

Anchorette didn't think that was a good idea. "Not yet. You know that the rehab centre said that you need support and need to take it slow, so no diving into something new, because I'm not allowing it, okay? In fact, forget the okay bit—it's not open to discussion."

Aine looked at her in shock. "Okay, again, what have you done with Anchorette, and who are you? Seriously, why you are never like this with Joe? If you stuck up for yourself more often, then maybe your relationship would be less complicated," Aine said, slightly concerned as to which direction the conversation would take next.

"Thank you there, Sherlock Holmes, but it's called compromising, and sometimes you have to back down—you know, the lose the battle to win the war theory," Anchorette said sharply, becoming frustrated by Aine commenting on her relationship.

"I was crap at history in school so I don't know what the hell you're on about there, but here is another theory for you—compromising is a two-way street, and all I see is a one-way, with it being his." Aine knew she had a point but wished she had held her tongue.

"You've got to give a little to get a little," Anchorette replied.

"So when do you get a little?" Aine replied back.

Anchorette went silent. She could see that this would end up getting nasty if she replied, so it was time to lose the battle again. "I'm going to check up on Keith. He has been asleep for a long while now, and he needs to be fed. Can you carry on cooking dinner while I go and see to him?" Anchorette didn't wait for a reply; she just walked out of the kitchen, frustrated. Here was Aine, who was getting Anchorette's support, knocking Joe and how he treated her, and yet Anchorette was the one in a committed marriage and Aine was not. Anchorette really wanted to let rip at her, but she knew she could not kick Aine down like that. She didn't want to undo all the progress that had been made. Plus, she didn't know if she was mad at Aine or at herself: Aine just might have had a small point about the whole giving-and-taking bit. All Anchorette knew was that she would avoid that talk and keep focused on Aine's recovery. Anchorette could not fail that part, even if Aine had been horrid to her.

The rest of the evening was spent in quietness, both of them unsure of how to express their feelings to each other and neither wanting to upset the other again. Anchorette hated going off to bed on a bad feeling and hoped that they could put it to one side and start anew.

Chapter Thirteen

Aine

A ine woke up early with Minstral purring gently on her lap. *He is the friendliest cat I have ever come across,* she thought. She lay there stroking him gently as not to disturb his slumber. She hadn't noticed at first until she turned to look at the clock on the wall that Grandmama Hartwood was sitting in Anchorette's nursing chair.

"He likes that," she said.

"How long have you been sitting there?" Aine asked. *She knows how I hate this whole situation of still seeing her.*

"Not long, just a few moments. How are you feeling today?" Grandmama Hartwood asked.

Aine was feeling better but she didn't want to acknowledge anything. "I'm still feeling a little shaky and unbalanced," she replied.

"You know, I always knew when my daughters lied to me, so I don't know why you are trying to lie to me now. Perhaps it's the ghostly thing, I don't know, but you should know for future reference that I can still detect it. Even in the afterlife. Now we have to start helping your sister. You know she is danger with that husband of hers, and you have to keep focused," Grandmama Hartwood said firmly.

"I know that now, but just how am I to break this to Anchorette? Suggestions would be helpful. It's not like I can bring it into a conversation one day—'So, how do you feel about hubby being a full-time assassin designed to impregnate you?'" Aine said with a raised eyebrow. "She will think I'm straight back on the drugs again, and that would be like golden ammunition to Joe, to have my ass kicked out permanently. And then what?" Aine's voice had gone up a few octaves with stress, and it had disturbed Minstral's sleep. He woke up meowing, a little disgruntled. He got up, looked in Grandmama Hardwood's direction, and meowed a friendly meow. "He can see you?" Aine asked.

"Yes, of course he can. Why do you think all pets bark and meow at what everyone else views as just thin air? They can see us—the good and the, well, not so good," Grandmama Hartwood said.

"Well, that's good to know, I guess," Aine said.

"Why don't you let fate take its course and go for a shower? You never know what surprises are around the corner," Grandmama Hartwood said, slowly fading.

It seemed so calm when she disappeared that way. It was very unsettling when she just popped in and out of thin air. Aine pulled back the covers and Minstral jumped off the bed and padded out of the room. She grabbed her dressing gown and headed towards the bathroom, preparing herself for a day to let fate take its course.

Chapter Fourteen

Anchorette

It was late when Joe came home. Anchorette looked at the alarm: it read 2.45 a.m. Although it was Friday and he had no work the following day, she felt really annoyed that he had been out that late. Joe was so drunk that he fell asleep on the bathroom floor, and Anchorette was determined that she was not going to move him. He would have been dead weight, and if he was going to be sick, he was at least in the right room and might aim in the right direction.

So it was a surprise when Anchorette awoke to the sound of Joe yelling. He sounded really angry. This confused her at first. *At whom and what is he shouting?* she thought. *Aine? Oh, hell!*

Anchorette quickly got up and ran to the hallway to see Aine giggling back into her bedroom and closing the door before bursting into a roar of laughter. Joe opened the bathroom door, ready to shout another mouthful of abuse to Aine's door, when he stopped and saw Anchorette standing there and looking at him. He was naked and looked like he had not only been dragged through the hedge backwards, but that the hedge had slam-dunked him and pulverized him, winning hands down. She tried hard to keep a straight face.

Joe knew that she wanted to laugh at him too. He slammed the bathroom door in anger, which in turn woke up Keith and made him start crying with fright. Anchorette sighed and, dragging her feet, went to see to Keith and comfort him. She took Keith downstairs and put on the baby channel for him to watch while she gently rocked him back and forth.

Aine came downstairs to the sitting room, where they looked at each other and giggled quietly. "Have to say, Anchorette, I don't see the attraction personally. I know I might be dead against going to rehab, but I am definitely going to be needing therapy for that shock. I think you're safe from girls chasing after him. If anyone else saw and smelt him first thing in the morning, they would be in need of a good shrink, too."

They giggled a little more. At least last night was all forgotten; they just had to compose themselves for the rest of the day and try to behave.

"Here, will you take Keith while I make a start on breakfast? He is still a little upset with the awakening he just had," Anchorette said. She passed Keith to Aine, and the two of them sat watching Mister Maker and his shapes. Keith liked the shapes and colours; they made him giggle a little. Anchorette heard him as she headed for the kitchen to make a fry-up. As Anchorette was finishing up breakfast, she heard Joe come down the stairs and walk into the sitting room where Aine and Keith were. Anchorette dished out the food, grabbed some cutlery and the plates of food, and headed back to the sitting room. Anchorette could hear that Joe's voice was slightly raised and hostile as he spoke to Aine.

"Give me Keith, now. He is my son, and you're not taking him away from me, you crackhead. You might have my wife convinced that you have changed, but I don't believe your act for one second. Now give me my son," Joe said with hatred in his voice.

"This is no act, Joe. I'm trying to go straight now, and as for me trying to take your wife away from you, just remember that first and foremost she is my sister and I will always be here for her, even when you're not, even when you're out meeting up with Lindsey. Say, how is that going? You two still meeting up whenever there happens to be a business meeting? Or have you managed other lame excuses?" Aine knew what Joe had been up to and had never told Anchorette any of it.

"That was a long time ago. I have not seen Lindsey since I found out that Anchorette was going to have Keith. She does not need to know, either, or I will tell her about the time you tried it on with me. It might not be true, but she will at least be hurt with you just as much as she would with me." Anchorette could not believe what she was hearing from Joe's mouth.

Aine replied, "Joe, we both know that it was you who tried it on with me, and the reason you don't like me is not because of addiction, it's because I knocked you back and wounded your ego. Now I'm going to keep a hold of Keith for a little while longer, because Anchorette asked me to look after him seeing as you were trying to sort yourself out from last night. Hot date, was it?" Aine asked in a sour tone.

If Joe did reply, Anchorette did not hear it. She had looked down and seen that she had forgotten to put the sauce on Joe's plate, so she went back to the kitchen, poured on some ketchup, and walked in with breakfast as though she had not heard anything, her face as straight as if she were playing poker. She wanted to get to the bottom of this and knew she could only ask Aine, as Joe had just shown that he would do anything to cover up a lie. *Plus*, she thought, *Aine is starting to owe me big time. Why did she have to come back and turn not just her life upside down but mine, too?*

Joe took his fry-up and then announced that he had to go out for the rest of the day, as he had to wrap up the business deal and he had no idea how long it would take. At that point Aine handed Keith to Anchorette, placed her breakfast on the floor, and excused herself, saying she had to tidy herself up before eating. So Anchorette took Keith and brought him into the kitchen for his breakfast.

Anchorette's head was still swimming with what she had just heard. She wanted to scream and yell at both of them, but she also knew that if she did, she would not get the answers that she needed and would totally lose focus.

Joe came through with his empty plate and kissed her while she had her back to him. He tried to cuddle her, but she was feeding Keith and did not want his hands anywhere near her, especially if he'd had his hands on Lindsey. Lindsey had been a bridesmaid at their wedding and was, she thought, one of her closest friends. It was starting to make sense to Anchorette why Lindsey had suddenly been offered a job in the city: it had been at about the same time that Anchorette had discovered that she was pregnant with Keith. *Oh, hell, what am I going to do? How am I going to face this?* After Joe left, Aine came downstairs and ate her breakfast. Anchorette decided to wait till Aine had finished to ask her.

Anchorette's breakfast was still sitting in the frying pan. Her stomach was so knotted up with dread that if she ate anything she might not be able to keep it down.

Aine walked in, complimenting her sister on a wonderful breakfast and placing her plate in the sink.

It was then that she noticed something was not right, but never got the chance to ask.

Chapter Fifteen

Anchorette

"So how long have Joe and Lindsey been having an affair?" Anchorette asked Aine outright. *There isn't much point in wasting time. Time to strike while the iron is hot and poking into my skull.*

Aine looked at Anchorette and then said, "You heard that? Why did you not say anything before?"

Okay, what the hell, Anchorette thought. *I didn't think I would be the one answering questions.* "Just tell me!" Anchorette snapped. "I want to know everything, and no holding back this time." Anchorette had snapped a little, but not fully: that bit she was saving for Joe. The hot poker stabbed a little further into her brain.

Aine was not expecting that reaction. She motioned for both of them to sit down at the table and then she took a breath, trying to collect her thoughts.

"Okay, do you remember when I decided that I was not coming to your wedding, and everyone thought it was because Mum had done a convincing job on me to not come and not let you and the family down?"

Anchorette nodded, her eyes narrowing at the shock that it went as far back as that.

Aine carried on. "Well, it was not because of Mum. I was living in the city, as you know, and it was the weekend. I was out with a group of friends—it was also the night that I met Brett, but this is not the time for that. I was at the bar ordering a round when I heard his voice. He had not seen me, or else he did not recognize me on the fact that I was wearing a neon pink wig, but I assumed that you would be with him. I was going to go over and give my reasons to you for not attending you wedding, so I followed him to his table. He was sitting with a woman, and, well, I knew it was not you because of the public display that was going on. I decided that I would confront him then and there, but Shelly had caught up with me and asked what was holding me up on the drinks, so I went back to the bar to get the drinks. I had every intention of going back to confront him, but when I did he was no longer there. So I decided that I should come back home and see if he would say anything, but I was never able to get a moment alone with him, and I had by then thought that it was just coincidence, that it was someone else who looked like him. Problem came when I decided to come to your wedding. I swear to you that I did not recognize Lindsey until she was walking down the aisle. You have no idea how much I wanted to rip her throat out there and then, but you looked so happy standing there. I was tempted when the priest asked if anyone knew why you two should not be together, but I didn't want to make a fool out of you—plus, you know what mother would have been like. So I did what I thought was best and cornered him after the ceremony. I let him know that I knew what he was like and that he was to end it straightaway, and he told me that he'd already had. I believed him. I even turned on Lindsey—I got her at the girls' toilet. He had not warned her of my knowledge, and I thought that I had definitely scared the hell out of her. I honestly thought that that was it until just over a year ago when I saw them both back in the city. It was at a tube station, and I followed them to a café. I saw Lindsey upset, and after she had left I confronted Joe again. He told me that he had just ended it and that you were pregnant with Keith. He told me not to say anything. He even tried to threaten me and hurt me, but you know that it takes a lot to scare me."

Aine was done. The red-hot pain was throbbing in Anchorette's head.

Anchorette sat numb for the rest of the day. She had not expected to hurt as much as she did. Now would be the perfect time to take up the vocation of a nun. She had the vow of silence down to an art. If Anchorette had joined the nunnery to begin with, then her marital life would have been plain and simple: she would have devoted herself to one mystery man who just happened to be perfect in every way and would never hurt her. She started to wonder about what the rules were for babies in the nunnery, and then realized that her mind was talking complete and utter crap. Plus, she could not picture herself in a habit and wimple. *Think, Anchorette, think.* She didn't know whether to confront him in a blazing row or let it slip by, given that the affair was now over. Was this all she was worth, being a second prize because she had fallen pregnant? Would Joe have ever run off with Lindsey?

That was it. That's what she would do. She would take Keith and go, but she needed to get the credit card that she shared with Joe. He always had it in his wallet, as he tended to use it for business meetings and always got paid back by the company, or so that's what he said. She knew she could never again believe another word he said.

By the time Anchorette started to come back to reality, the shadows had moved to the other side of the room and the sun was beginning to set. Anchorette got up and went to find Keith and Aine; they were both outside in the back garden. Aine was humming to Keith when she turned around and saw Anchorette standing there. Anchorette gave her a halfhearted smile—that's all she could manage.

Aine went over to her with Keith, gave her a hug, and said, "At least you have cried it out now. I thought you were never going to stop. It even frightened Keith a little, so we have just stayed out of your way all day. How are you feeling? I know that's a stupid question, but we are only human to ask."

Anchorette looked at her and asked, "Have I been crying all day? I hadn't even noticed that the day had gone by," Anchorette said, confused.

"You were crying a lot. You would go quiet, and just when I thought you were all cried out, you cried even more," Aine said in a very protective way, knowing that Anchorette had to get it out of her system but hating the fact that she was the one who had made her cry.

"Don't do anything and don't say anything, okay? I'm going to fix it. We are leaving tomorrow once Joe has gone out—I will send him out to do an errand or something. We have to pack clothes, just the bare essentials. Do you think you could fit some of Keith's things in with yours?" Anchorette asked.

"We go tonight?" Aine asked, worried by the sudden rashness that was coming from her sister.

"No, it will have to be tomorrow. I need to sneak into his wallet and get the credit card that we share, and then we can go. I have no money otherwise, apart from what's in the bank account, but that won't get us through to where I want to go," Anchorette answered.

Aine looked puzzled. Anchorette knew that Aine had never seen her like this, so emotionally switched off. But as feelings right now went, getting too emotional would tip her over into a complete nervous wreck, and she had to be strong and get Keith out of this.

"Okay, but I don't like this. Are you going to be all right sharing a bed with him tonight?" Aine asked.

"I will have to be. We need to start packing stuff now before he gets home. I have no idea what time he will be home—when it comes to his meetings out of work, they can take hours," Anchorette said, beginning to make plans.

"Anchorette, I have one question to ask," Aine said while they quickly walked back into the house and back up the stairs. "Where is it you're planning on taking us?"

Anchorette spun around at the top of the stairs with Keith in her arms.

"We are going to Canada," Anchorette answered. "You have a passport, right?"

"Yeah, I have one, but why there?" Aine asked, puzzled.

"Because we are going to live a dream. I'm going to set up a business in selling cactus plants. I have always wanted to do that since—"

Aine finished off the sentence: "Since you were a little girl. Okay, we live the dream and no more mistakes. We both start afresh." They were both on the same page again, and it was good.

Chapter Sixteen

Anchorette

Once they had packed the stuff they would need and Anchorette had put Keith to sleep, they hugged each other and headed off to bed. It was late, about 12.30 a.m., when Joe got in. He was not as drunk as Anchorette had hoped he would be, which was odd for him.

He crept into bed, putting his arm around her. To Anchorette it felt creepy knowing that he had been with her and that he could be with someone else and not even care about her feelings. She wanted to kick him there and then and hurt him where it would count most. Put him out of action permanently. But then were would that put Keith? His father would have sole custody and Anchorette did not want that. She had to act together. This was going to be harder than she thought, and she would have to dig deep to find the strength to keep the act up one more night.

Anchorette had no idea what he had in mind, though it quickly became clear that Joe wanted to have sex with her, as he kept trying to wake her up. Anchorette blocked out what he did to her. She just went through the motions, pleasing him, giving him what he wanted, thinking that this time tomorrow she would be on a flight to Canada with Aine and Keith starting a new life. She may as well use him just as much as he used her: let him think that everything was still all good and that no one could make her feel the way she did but him. She wondered if Joe had ever had farewell sex with Lindsey or with any other woman. Who knew how many others there have been? Just then she remembered what Aine and Joe had talked about that morning, that Joe had tried with Aine. Anchorette wondered if they had had sex, and had to keep reminding herself that Aine had told him that she was the one who had rejected him. But Anchorette did wonder how many there were.

She tried to concentrate on pleasing him. She could not let him think that she was distracted, and so they carried on. It was not like she imagined it would be. There was no happy, satisfied feeling of getting one over him. If anything, she felt sick to the core. But after she cuddled up to him, she could feel a tear or two falling down her face. They were silent tears. She could not tell if they were tears of happiness of a new life around the corner or tears of sadness for the way Joe had lied to her over the years.

The following morning Anchorette got up early and went downstairs to grab Joe's wallet. It was on the table where he had left it the night before. She found the joint bank account card pretty easily and quickly put his wallet back on the table. She placed the small piece of freedom in her back pocket. Her hands were starting to sweat but she had to keep calm: she was a little bit closer to her dream.

Anchorette went into the kitchen and looked in the fridge. *Damn, I thought I had enough milk, but obviously not.* She grabbed the keys and slipped out quietly to the corner shop. It was not far, and this was not the first time that Anchorette had gone to see Mr. Harding so early in the morning to stock up on some much-needed items for breakfast, as when she was pregnant she had been very forgetful. With that memory of forgetfulness, Anchorette realized that she had left the house without her purse. "Oh, hell," Anchorette muttered as she turned about and headed back to the house. She slipped the keys into the lock as quietly as she could: she did not want to wake anyone up just yet. But once inside, Anchorette could already hear voices. One was Joe's, and it sounded pretty angry.

The first thought that went through Anchorette's mind was, *Oh, hell, what has Aine gone and done?* But as she went upstairs to see what was happening, she could hear Aine crying, which was unlike her. Anchorette walked carefully to the bedroom door and saw through the crack between the door and the frame that Joe was leaning over Aine, who was tied to the bed frame by her wrists. Anchorette, confused, wondered what the hell Joe was doing.

"You know I should have done this a long time ago and put your parents and Anchorette out of their misery. You came back into my life like a poisonous snake and tried to take all the attention. You stole my wife and son and now you're planning on moving back into the area, waiting for my wife to set you up in a cosy flat with money that I have earned for my family. And then you threatened yesterday to tell her about Lindsey and me. Well, enough. No more." Anchorette wondered why Aine had not said anything, but Joe was blocking her view and it was only when he moved a little that she saw what was in his hand. It was a syringe filled with what looked like brown stuff.

Shocked, Anchorette gasped, and that was when Joe realized that she was at the bedroom door. He lunged at

Aine, who was gagged and could not scream, and tried to put the syringe in her vein.

Anchorette ran in, not sure what she was going to do. All she knew was that she could not let him put that in Aine's arm. Anchorette ran directly towards Joe, picking up a foot stool on the way in. She aimed and threw it at him. It knocked the syringe out of his hand, but it also left Anchorette defenceless. Joe looked at his wife with rage in his eyes, and that was when Anchorette knew the game was up. Joe got up and went to grab Anchorette but missed. She turned to run down the stairs, but he managed to grab hold of her long caramel hair. Anchorette might have made it to the second step when she felt the yank. She lost her footing, and Joe dragged her backwards to their bedroom. He flung her like a rag doll onto the bed, but Anchorette was not going down without a fight. She kicked him hard in the leg, which made him stumble back. Anchorette managed to get off the bed but suddenly Joe was there in front of her again. He grabbed her by her left arm and pulled her back onto the bed. She tried to bite him on the hands, but he was too strong. Joe then picked her up off the bed, lifted her into the air, and threw her up against the wardrobe. She flew straight into the wardrobe's glass doors. All Anchorette was conscious of was the sound of glass shattering into tiny pieces. Joe then grabbed her and picked her up again, putting Anchorette face-first onto the bed. She thought that he was going to rape her, but he didn't. He ripped open her shirt at the back, and she could not understand what he was doing or why.

"You're supposed to be my wife, you slag. Why the hell are you overprotecting that slut in the other room? I thought you were different from her, I thought we could have a life together, but how can we when she will always be in our way?"

Anchorette, frightened and confused, didn't understand what he meant. She had all but devoted herself to him in this marriage, and he had been the one who had run off with another woman. That was when she decided that if she was going to suffer, so was he.

"I'm a slag when it was you who was having the affair with Lindsey?" Anchorette choked out, muffled by the bedding.

That made things even worse. What else should she have expected? Joe bent down next to the broken glass and picked up a piece. At first she thought Joe might slash his wrists, but oh no, he stood over Anchorette and dug the glass into her back. She could not see what he was doing but it hurt a lot. She started to scream but he pushed her face into the bedding to muffle the sound. Then he started scraping into her back again. It was like he was carving something. The pain was too much and Anchorette passed out.

The next thing she knew she was waking up. She thought she might be in a clean hospital bed, but then she could not understand why she was in so much pain and why her back was sticky and wet. The other strange thing was that she could feel movement. Maybe she was in an ambulance? But when Anchorette fully woke up and looked around, all she saw was Joe driving the car along the motorway. She realized she was lying in the backseat of their car.

"Where are we going?" she asked Joe, but he stayed focused on the road like he was on autopilot and she was not there. It was then that she knew the end was in sight. He was going to kill her and dump her somewhere. But where? From their surroundings she realized he was taking her to a forest where they used to have romantic picnics. They would be turning off the motorway soon. No one would ever find her. If she was ever going to save Keith from this, she had to act fast.

Anchorette's hands were tied together, but she managed to start to unwind the window. The pain down her back became even more excruciating, but she managed to wind it down without him noticing. Anchorette then braced herself for the next bit: undo the seat belt and hurl herself out the window. Yes, she might die from it, but there would be no way he would get away with what he had done. Anchorette looked around. There was no sign of Keith in the car; that was good, as she would have lost all courage if she had seen his face one last time.

Anchorette went to grab for the buckle on the seat belt, but Joe noticed that she was about to do something and grabbed both her hands. He turned to look at her, his eyes cold and dead. He hated her. She pulled his hand up to her mouth and bit it as hard as she could. Joe let go and Anchorette went straight for the seat belt again. Success. She heard the click, which was all she needed. She started to lift herself out the window, but Joe grabbed her again, and while he was pulling her back into the seat, Joe did not see the lorry in front of him start to slow down. Just as Anchorette was being forced back into the seat, the car smashed into the back of the lorry.

Oh, hell, not more glass, was all Anchorette thought as she headed towards the windscreen. Her hands went up to try to break the glass instead of her face. Her eyes were shut and again she could hear the sound of glass shattering. She hated it so much: that tinkling sound should have sounded nice but in reality it sounded like death trying to kill her.

Anchorette landed on the bonnet of the car. She felt a different kind of pain this time: it was going through her stomach, and she could also feel pain in the lower part of her back. She tried to get up and couldn't figure out why she couldn't move. All she heard was screaming. Anchorette didn't know if the screaming was coming from her or from other people. Traffic had screeched to a halt and people were getting out of their cars to help. They looked shocked to see her laying there. Finally she heard a different type of screaming: it came from the sound of ambulances and fire engines rushing to get her the help she needed most desperately. Anchorette's last thought before she passed out was that she was safe at last from Joe.

Chapter Seventeen

Anchorette

Anchorette awoke to the sound of machinery whirling and humming and could feel something on her face. She went to make a grab at it but a hand stopped her. *Oh god, please don't let that be Joe,* she thought. Anchorette carefully opened her eyes to see Aine smiling down at her. Anchorette was so glad to see her.

"Oh, no you don't. You keep that oxygen tube there, it's helping you. And if you think about pulling that drip out of your wrist, then you will have me to deal with, okay?"Aine said with gentleness and caring that was reflected on her face.

Anchorette found it difficult to talk, as a tube had been put down her throat to help her breathe. The operation she had gone through had been very serious. The doctors thought there may be lasting damage. When she had landed on the bonnet of the car her body had been punctured by a large piece of shattered glass. Luckily it had just missed her kidney and lung, but it had exposed her intestines and pinned her down, preventing her from moving.

Janet and David came to visit. Janet didn't stay for too long: she could not bear to look Anchorette in the eyes, as she knew she had been in the wrong. David agreed with Janet when she insisted that Anchorette sign Keith over to her instead of letting him go into foster care. Anchorette was about to agree when Janet blamed everything on Aine's return. That was when Anchorette decided enough was enough.

After that Anchorette drifted in and out of sleep for the rest of that day. The following day was a bit clearer; the doctors were pleased with Anchorette's progress and reduced some of her medication. At visiting hour Aine explained what had happened.

"After you stopped screaming I thought he had killed you, but you must have just passed out. He then came back into my room. Keith was awake by then and was crying a lot and if I could have gotten to him I would have, but he had me tied up. He turned me over and my arms were crossed. He ripped off my nightshirt and with a piece of glass started carving into my back. It was not till after I had arrived that the surgeon who stitched me together told me he had done the same to you. He had carved the word 'slag' on your back and the word 'slut' on mine. He then thought I had passed out. I heard him making a comment about how weak and pathetic you were because you had passed out. That gave me hope. He left the room but then I heard him dragging something. I now know that it must have been you. He took you to the car. I was not sure what he was going to do with me or Keith, so I just stayed quiet till I heard the car engine start, and then I got up onto my knees and pulled the gag off my mouth and waited till he was definitely out of earshot and screamed for all I had. I thought that between Keith and myself we could get some attention.

"It didn't take long for the police to arrive, and once I had explained to them what had happened they put out across the radio to start looking for his car. The police officers took us to the hospital. Keith is fine, but with me having had surgery and the doctors also helping me go through detox, the social workers won't risk me having him. "Aine looked at Anchorette, waiting to see if there would be a response, but Anchorette kept quiet, waiting for Aine to finish telling her what had happened. Aine cleared her throat and continued more softly. "A while later we heard that the car had been involved in a crash, but I didn't know how bad it was. Mum and Dad had by then turned up—they wanted to take Keith home and were blaming all of it on me. I was not about to take the blame for Joe, so I told them what had happened. Mum still wanted to blame me, so I took the padding off my back to show them both what Joe had done, but still they blamed it on me and said that some druggie ex had something to do with all of this. It was not until Mum saw you and Joe coming in on stretchers that she realized that I had been telling the truth, because Joe by then was trying to go for Mum and Dad and the police had to cuff him to the bed. He has been taken away to the prison hospital—he just had bruises, nothing too serious apart from his ego being wounded. I told the police officers that I was more than happy to stand trial even if you're not well enough to get out of hospital. I hope the judge gives him life for what he has done to us both."

Aine started to cry. It was strange that in only a short space of time Anchorette had seen her cry twice. It had been one of her last memories before hitting the windscreen.

Anchorette cleared her throat to speak. "It's not your fault, Aine," Anchorette said, trying to comfort her as best she could.

Aine wiped her tears away and said, "I should make a move and go see how Keith is doing, as I am usually leaving about this time. The social workers have agreed that a familiar face is good for Keith to see, but I will come back later in the evening and see how you are. You take it easy and I will see you later." Aine bent down carefully to give Anchorette a kiss on the forehead; it hurt Aine as much as movement hurt Anchorette.

After Aine left the room, Anchorette cried all the hour till a nurse came in and gave her a light sedative to help her sleep. She didn't want it, as she just wanted to hide from the memories and make the pain to go away, though she knew that when she next awoke it would all still be there.

Later that evening, Anchorette slowly came to. She fell asleep again and woke the next day to the sound of a familiar voice shouting in the hallway; the drugs the nurse had given her had knocked her right out for the whole night. Aine walked in, looking more than a little peeved, but when she saw her sister sitting up alert and awake, her face changed to a smile, which was more comforting to see.

"Who was that out there with you?" Anchorette asked, because there was no way that she could not have heard it.

"Oh, it was just a hospital porter. He banged into me with his trolley and it caught my leg. It hurts still a little but I bet nothing compared to how you are feeling," Aine said, trying to change the subject.

Anchorette may have still been on medication to keep the pain away, but she somehow knew that something was up. "I'm not stupid, you know. I may just have been in a crash and have been battling to save my life, but I still know when you're lying to me. I can tell you are," Anchorette said, not pretending to be fooled.

Aine walked around the bed and said calmly, "It's nothing, really. Just some old mates wanting to catch up and hang out, but I told them that now is not the time and I am not interested, that's all." Aine took her sister's hand and smiled. "For a second I was really tempted but I chose not to."

Anchorette still was not sure but smiled back. She asked Aine to go get the nurse, as she was in a little discomfort. The drugs were wearing off, and she was starting to have difficulties in breathing and pain was spreading across her stomach. While Aine was away, Anchorette had more time to think clearly. She felt that something was up with Aine, and while she was not quite sure what it was, she knew that she had to focus on getting stronger and getting Aine and Keith out of the country and safe.

The nurse walked in with a smile. She was soon followed by Aine, who clearly disliked her, as she was pulling faces behind her back. It hurt when Anchorette tried to laugh discreetly, but hurt even more when she tried not to laugh at all. Aine saw this, and when she realized it, she stopped. The nurse checked all of Anchorette's tubes; she had been all that time pretending that they were not there at all, as it made her feel sick just thinking about it. The nurse then told Anchorette that the doctor would be down in a little while to talk to her about the operation and what the outcome of it would be. It all sounded very odd to Anchorette. *It must still be the drugs*, she thought. Outcome and the what-would-be: couldn't she just get a "You came close to dying a few times but hey, you're still kicking about and you get to take away a couple scars which will make you look freakish, but on the plus side you won't have to dress up for Halloween." Guess not. Aine told Anchorette that she was going to get a bite to eat and would be back to see her and the doc.

The doctor came in before Aine got back. In a weird sort of way he was good-looking. He was about five-foot-seven, of medium build and with balding hair, and very professional-looking. He was serious and got straight to the point without sugarcoating his words.

"So you're telling me that you had to cut my smaller intestine up because it was torn to shreds from the impact of me landing on the glass, and that for the time being I have to shit into a bag?" The doctor could see by Anchorette's facial expression that she was trying to remain calm; however, her heart rate monitor was not as calm as her face was. The machine was beeping a little too fast, and if it went any faster, it would keep up with the sirens of the ambulances that drove below outside.

"Please, you have to remain calm or I will have to sedate you, which would not be good for you right now given your condition," the doctor said.

"Half my intestine is in the bin and I have to crap in a bag. I think I'm entitled to be just a little bit upset, don't you think? I mean, is this permanent, or will you operate again to put all right?"

The doctor's face grew even tenser, and just then Aine walked in. He seemed to relax.

"Hi, I'm Anchorette's sister Aine."

The doctor introduced himself as Doctor Sullivan. Anchorette was worrying about the outcome and would not remember it.

Doctor Sullivan was not done; he carried on with more news. "There is something else that needs to be explained to you before we try to put all your intestines back in. I thought you would have already known, given that you are about five weeks now."

Anchorette's face looked a picture, because she could not understand a single word of what he was prattling on about. Aine's face was a mirror image.

"I'm sorry, but you have lost us with this talk. Five weeks what?" Anchorette asked.

The doctor's face dropped down; he wasn't sure how to spit it out, but he didn't have to. Aine picked up what he was about to say and blurted out, "Oh shit, girl, you're pregnant! When the hell did you last have a period and sex?" Anchorette's mind was such a blur that words were not even making sentences in her brain. Now she felt like the one speaking a foreign language, and oh boy, it was slapping her hard. Anchorette leaned to the right side of her bed and threw up.

Chapter Eighteen

Anchorette

After the doctor left and the nurse finished making Anchorette more comfortable, Anchorette asked Aine a question that she was not expecting. "Who were you talking to in thecorridor earlier? And don't try to deny it was about drugs."

Aine sat down on the bed and sighed. She had a faraway look in her eyes as if she was looking for the answer. She nodded her head once and then looked slightly to the left of Anchorette's shoulder, shaking her head.

"What exactly—or should I say who exactly—are you looking at over my shoulder, Aine?" Anchorette asked.

"Okay, okay, promise you're not going to freak out or anything," Aine said, smiling just a little.

Anchorette cocked an eyebrow and waited. Her reply was calm and simple. "I've done enough freaking out over the last forty-eight hours. What else have you got to throw in my direction?"

"Okay, here goes," Aine said, taking a deep breath. "You remember back when we were kids and Auntie Hettie and Grandma died in that fire? Well, it wasn't the fire that killed them. The fire was set to cover the murderers' tracks and to make their deaths look accidental, which they weren't. Some professionals killed them just after we left that day, and now they are tracking us, or at least trying to," Aine said, a little more serious.

"Wait up, hold on a sec. You're talking to Gran and Aunt Hettie?" Anchorette squealed, a little shocked.

"Yes, and Grandma ain't happy about being called Gran." Aine breathed a little more freely, relieved that that was the only reaction Anchorette had given her.

Anchorette looked over her shoulder and whispered, "Sorry, Grandma."

Aine shook her head in disbelief. "Okay, Aunt Hettie, I'm getting to it. Sorry, Anchorette. Aunt Hettie is having a go at me because she wants me to tell you the rest. The trackers are trying to track us both, but they can't because you don't have your talent. You married a mortal, and when you marry a mortal your powers remain dormant," Aine said, looking slightly to the left of where she had been looking before.

"Okay, back it up a little. Tracking, mortals, my talent? Slowly explain," Anchorette said.

Aine huffed just a little. "All right. Remember when we would go stay at Grandmama's and she and Aunt Hettie would teach us cool things that our mum disliked?" Aine pushed on, not waiting for an answer. "Well, that's because what they were telling us was all true. They were witches, and it's in our bloodline to be, too. When we were born we were born with a talent, as well as the natural ability to heal slightly faster than the average human. My talent is that I can speak to spirits—also known as necromancy. I don't like it all the time, especially not in a hospital—there are a lot of spirits around here, to say the least. Your talent no longer exists because you married Joe, a mortal."

"Ah, but that will soon not make any difference, as I intend to divorce him."

Aine shook her head. "It doesn't work that way. You made a binding contract—divorce is not recognized in our practise. Only if you find true happiness and fall in love will it break, and then the trackers will find us easily," Aine said.

Anchorette looked stunned. "I can't possibly fall in love again. It's hard enough trying to find one man, let alone another, and in my given condition I'm crapping in a bag. They are not going to drop at my feet. I think you can safely say we are well off the trackers' radar."

Aine looked a little to her right. "Not necessarily. Grandma says it would be safer for us to move to a place far away. I have active powers so they can still track me. If you remember, after I moved in with you I didn't want to go out, and that was why."

Anchorette looked at Aine. "Is this for real? How do we handle this on top of everything else we are going through right now?"

Aine had a faraway look on her face. She looked in the direction of the window and snapped, "Look, I ain't got time to help you find your white fuzzy light."

Aine turned back to Anchorette, who was looking at her with a raised eyebrow, and asked, "What?"

Anchorette looked back at her and said, "That was rude, but getting back to our problem, or should I say problems, what do we do and where do we go?"

Aine sat at the end of Anchorette's bed as gently and carefully as she could to minimize any jostling. She looked deep in thought, and said, "You remember that daft childhood dream of yours of living in Canada and opening a plant shop that specialises in cacti? How about we do it?"

"You're kidding, right? That was just a childhood fantasy," Anchorette said, shaking her head in disbelief and regretting it just as soon as she had.

"No, I'm not kidding. It would work, Aunt Hettie is confident," Aine said, looking a little farther left than she had the first time.

Anchorette's breathing had become rapid; her head was trying to process so much information, and she was trying to get through her pain. First up she had to know what or who the hell a tracker was.

"Aine, what's a tracker?" Anchorette asked. She could see that Aine was still in heavy talks with her Grandmama and Aunt Hettie. The fact that Aine was talking to either of them was a lot to take in, but not totally unexpected. Anchorette recalled how Aine would at times just shut off from the rest of the world and distance herself from everyone, including herself. Why would a tracker want to kill Grandmama and Aunt Hettie? What had they done that was so wrong or bad? Anchorette could not recall seeing anything wrong or bad when she visited them as a child.

"Sorry. Grandmama and Aunt Hettie were just explaining that they sensed a tracker close by, but what with this being a hospital and full of spirits, as long as I shut off for a while the trackers will go. Grandmama and Aunt Hettie will let me know when it's safe for me to leave," Aine said.

"Okay, so you have some time on your hands to explain to me what and who a tracker is and why we—or should I say you—are being targeted," Anchorette said sharply. Aine could tell that Anchorette was trying to remain calm and process it all.

"Well?" Anchorette asked impatiently.

"Okay, okay, technically the trackers work for a company called the DSS," Aine said, cocking her head to the side.

"So the government is involved in this somehow?" Anchorette asked sarcastically.

Aine grinned, as she had made the same conclusion when Aunt Hettie told her the same thing. "You have no idea as to how silly I just saw myself look there. No, it's not the government. This DDS are a completely different sort of life-suckers altogether. From what Aunt Hettie has explained, DSS stands for Dark Shadow Slayers. It is run by humans and protected by a dark force of sorts. Trackers are just the beginning of it—they're sort of the pawns in a game of chess. Their leader and commanders send trackers into the world to find us and kill us. They want to get rid of us all. It's been happening for years. They have operated at different times over the centuries. Some were more noticeable and were written down in history, but most of it has been covered up or buried and forgotten. Grandmama and Aunt Hettie did their best to stay under the radar, but somehow a tracker found them, and, well, we don't really need to go there on that bit," Aine, said waiting for Anchorette's reaction. They both remembered the night the police turned up.

"Well, that really does add a whole new meaning to signing on down at the DSS," Anchorette said after a moment's thought. Aine tried to muffle her laughter, but Anchorette could feel the vibration going through the bed and winced a little.

"Sorry, but that was kinda funny," Aine said, trying to get her laughter under control.

"Okay, so why are they not tracking Mum then? Or are they? Is she in danger?" Anchorette asked, a little frightened for her mother. Although Janet had been horrible, she didn't wish any harm on her. Aine didn't quite feel the same but answered her anyway.

"No, Mum had asked Grandmama to remove her talents when she was in her teens and to wipe her memory clear. Mum had the same talent as me, as it turned out, but Mum didn't like it or couldn't handle it. When we become teenagers our talents start to come on stronger and we get a choice. Unfortunately, because Mum didn't remember anything, after Grandmama and Aunt Hettie were killed, we were sort of left to defend ourselves. But by all accounts we have done very well in hiding from the trackers. Aunt Hettie told me that me taking drugs not only suppressed my use of my talent, but also threw the trackers off my scent. It somehow masked them from pinpointing me. No such luck now. Also, when Grandmama cast a spell to remove Mum's talent, it gave her protection," Aine said.

They sat there for a while, Aine letting Anchorette process the news and take it all in. Anchorette drifted in and out of sleep until late evening, when the nurse brought Anchorette her dinner.

Chapter Nineteen

Anchorette

With so much information coming at Anchorette, she felt emotionally and physically drained. Aine excused herself so Anchorette could eat in peace, leaving the TV switched on to keep her company.

While Anchorette sat and contemplated all the information she had taken on that afternoon and whether it was safe to eat the soup of the day, which was a brownish, reddish colour, the phone next to her rang. Anchorette had forgotten that it was there and was slightly startled. She winced slightly as she leant over to pick up the receiver and cleared her throat as best she could. "Hello," Anchorette answered.

"Hello, Anchorette, it's your mum," Janet said and then quickly pushed on, asking her, "How are you? Are you doing well?"

Anchorette was surprised. Of all the people it could be, she had not been expecting it to be her mother. She felt a pang of guilt: after today's revelations, she just wasn't sure how to feel towards Janet anymore.

"I'm doing well, Mum. I'm making good progress, so the doctors say," Anchorette answered, trying to reach out in hope.

"Well, that's good. You know I feel really guilty about how things were left. Are you sure we could not help out with Keith, at least? You know I hate the thought of him being all alone in the system when your father and I could take him home with us." Anchorette knew what her mum meant. She hated that her son was in temporary foster care.

"You know he isn't really alone, Mum. Aine visits him daily, and the doctors say I'm making really fast progress." *But not fast enough*, Anchorette thought with a tear welling up in her eye.

"You know I don't think it's such a good idea to let Aine so close to Keith, Anchorette. She is not the most stable of people. Plus, I don't think Joe would like it much," Janet said.

Anchorette breathed in sharply. "You have spoken to Joe?" Anchorette asked, feeling shaken and completely off-balance. The offer of hope was slipping out of her grasp.

"He called this afternoon. You know you pushed him to it, as you know what Aine can be like. She has a knack for always ruining people's lives," Janet said, defending Joe.

"Mum, it was not Aine's fault. He did this all on his own," Anchorette said, the tear flowing down her cheek and the hope completely gone.

"Don't be so silly, Anchorette. The best and only choice you have is to drop all charges and patch things up with Joe. You know you will never make it on your own with Keith, and with Aine holding you down as well," Janet said harshly. "Don't be a silly child, Anchorette."

Anchorette was mad now. She was sick of being put down and told she wouldn't make it. She snapped, "You're wrong, mother. I am going to make it. All four of us are going to make it, and Joe can rot in jail," Anchorette said.

"All four? What do you mean, all four?" Janet asked, confused. Anchorette realized her mistake as soon as Janet picked it up.

"Anchorette, are you pregnant?" Janet asked.

"That has nothing to do with you, and neither does Keith. Good-bye, mother. Please don't call me here again," Anchorette said, the tears flowing faster down her face. She heard her mother shouting on the other end of the line as she put the receiver down.

Anchorette began to panic now. Fear became stronger and she sat there with her dinner growing cold in front of her. A little while later Aine came back. She saw Anchorette's face and knew that she had been crying.

"I know the hospital food is bad, but really, is it that bad?" Aine asked, trying to make a light joke.

"Mum called and I slipped, Aine. She knows that I'm pregnant, and she was talking to Joe this afternoon. She pleaded with me to go back to him, saying that I couldn't make it on my own and that you would hold me down. I didn't mean to, but I was so shocked and she caught me off-guard. I didn't think she would ever call here or speak to me again. I was prepared and I felt so guilty after what you had told me about Mum and her talent. She knows, Aine. What am I going to do if she tells Joe?" Anchorette sobbed with stricken fear. Aine went to her and hugged her.

"I'm not sure what we can and cannot do just yet. We have to get you better before we do anything. We should wait till tomorrow and see what your doctor says, and then make our plans," Aine said.

"Will you stay here with me tonight? I don't want to be alone." Anchorette hiccupped between sobs.

"Of course I will," Aine said, thinking of how Anchorette had been there for her only a few weeks ago now. "I'm not going anywhere, sis," she said soothingly and gently before letting go of the embrace. She took Anchorette's hand in one of hers, and with the other helped Anchorette to wipe away her tears.

Chapter Twenty

Aine

Aine was woken up by her phone vibrating on the side of the bed unit. She grabbed it as she got out of the hospital chair.

"Hello," she answered quietly.

"Hello, this is Detective Hampton. We spoke at the hospital a few days ago when I took a statement from you about your brother-in-law and sister."

Aine knew full well who he was. She still remembered seeing a younger Hampton standing in the sitting room and telling her mother the news of Grandmama and Aunt Hettie all those years ago.

"Yes, Detective, how can I help you?" she asked, walking out into the hallway. The nurses were doing their morning duties and preparing for the day ahead. Two of them were walking in her direction with towels in their hands. She nodded at them, noticing that they were going to wake up Anchorette and give her a bed bath.

"I would like to talk to you a little more about your brother-in-law and see if we have everything we need to make a conviction that will stick," Detective Hampton said.

"Um, sure. When would you like me to come down? I have been a bit tied up at the hospital, and on top of that the social workers are being difficult in letting me have access to my nephew Keith," Aine said, hoping he might help her a little.

Of course he didn't answer as far as Keith went. "If you wouldn't mind coming down to the station, anytime today would be fine. Just ask for me at the front desk and they will let me know that you are here. We would also like to talk to you about someone else that you perhaps knew, a Mr. Brett Hunter. His family gave us reason to believe that you were the last person to have contact with him before his disappearance, and we would like to get your version of what happened."

Aine swallowed, knowing that this would be one secret she couldn't hide for much longer. "Okay, I will come down this afternoon after I go back to the house to pick up some clothes for myself and Anchorette," Aine said.

"Of course, if it is easier for you, I could meet you at the house," Detective Hampton suggested, making it clear that she couldn't avoid him.

"Yes, that would be easier for me, thank you," Aine said, determined to not let him think she had something to hide.

"Shall see you then this afternoon," Detective Hampton said before hanging up. The line went dead and Aine leaned up against the wall in the corridor. She took some deep breaths and readied herself to go back in to speak to Anchorette. The nurses were there with the curtain around the bed for some privacy.

"Anchorette, it's me, Aine. I just had a phone call from Detective Hampton—he needs to speak to me this afternoon at the house, so I will have to go soon. Would you like me to pick up some fresh clothing for you?" Aine asked, waiting for a response.

There was nothing, no noise at all. Then the curtain rustled and the two nurses came out from behind it and ran towards the window. They tried to open the window but it wouldn't open quickly enough, so they ran past Aine, knocking her over, and went out the door and into the corridor. Aine heard their stomping footsteps fade as she regained her balance and went to see Anchorette. Anchorette lay on the bed motionless. Aine ran out into the corridor, horrified, and screamed for help.

Chapter Twenty-One

Aine

Aine paced up and down the corridor, waiting for anything. Aunt Hettie materialized just in front of her. "She will be fine," Aunt Hettie said.

Aine nodded, not wanting to speak and look silly. She pulled out her mobile phone and pretended to talk. "We should meet up back at the house," Aine said, speaking into her phone but looking right at Aunt Hettie.

"Okay, I will let Mum know that we are to see you there," Aunt Hettie said before fading away.

Aine put the phone away; she hadn't realized her hands were shaking. The police arrived not too long after, along with Detective Hampton.

"Okay, I want one of you to stand guard at all times here until we catch the person who is behind all of this. Aine, if you would, please come with me so we can get the details from you again," Detective Hampton said, looking at her and gesturing for her to follow. She did reluctantly, but it was of comfort to know that the officers were there. Then it hit her: Aunt Hettie had not said that Anchorette's baby would be fine as well. Tears trickled down her face as she followed the detective into an unoccupied room. He closed the door and motioned for her to take a seat in one of the chairs next to the empty bed. She sat as he took out his notebook and pen and positioned himself precariously on the edge of the bed. He looked down at her and, seeing her tears, let out a small sigh.

He gave her a moment to compose herself. She looked up at him and he nodded, knowing that she wouldn't say much till she was calmer.

He stood back up, wandered towards the table by the side of the bed, and found a box of tissues. He passed them to her. She grabbed a handful and wiped her tears away. He sat back down on the bed with the pen and notebook in his hands.

"Better?" he asked.

Aine nodded, not wanting to test her voice as she was only semi-composed.

"Okay, then. I need you to take me back as to what happened. Try to remember as much information as you can. The more you tell me now, the easier it will be for us to catch this person," he said, and then waited for her answer.

"I was on the phone with you. When I left Anchorette's room, she was still sleeping. We'd had a difficult night and she didn't want me to leave her all alone. Our mother had called her. She had blamed Anchorette for taking me in and helping me, and said that everything that had happened was somehow my fault. So I had stayed overnight. When you called, I left as to not disturb her. I was standing in the corridor just outside her room. The nurses were up and about doing their jobs. I noticed two nurses coming towards me, each with a towel in her hand. I didn't think anything of it, and nodded to them as they walked on in. Once we were finished talking I walked back in, assuming that Anchorette was getting a bed bath. I explained that I was going home soon and that if she liked I could pick her up some clean clothing, nightshirts and such. There was no response. The next thing I knew, the two women rushed out from the behind the curtain. It was closed—I thought for privacy. They ran to the window and tried to unlock it, but it wouldn't budge. Then they both pushed me as they ran out into the corridor. I saw Anchorette just laying there and instantly knew something was wrong, so I screamed out into the corridor for help. Then I was shoved out of the room by a nurse, and you turned up," Aine said. She was still wiping her tears away and took some more tissues to blow her nose.

"Can you describe what either woman looked like? Hair, eye colour, height, weight? Anything to help us?" He waited while Aine thought for a bit.

"The corridor was lit only by the early morning light, but they both had dark brown hair, shoulder-length, one straight and the other curly. About five-foot-seven, but not taller than that. They were both slim, a bit heavier than me but still slim. Both were white," Aine said, thinking about both of them. One of them had looked familiar, but she couldn't figure out how.

"Anything else?" the detective asked.

Aine shook her head. "No, I can't remember much else. I was talking to you at the time, so I was distracted. Do you know if Anchorette is going to be all right? The nurses won't tell me anything," Aine said.

"Just hang on a second, we are not done here. Is this in any way related to Mr. Hunter's family?" Detective Hampton asked Aine.

She looked him in the eye and answered firmly, "No." She carried on looking at him and he nodded.

"So it has to do with Joe somehow then?" he asked her again.

"It's a possibility. I honestly don't know. Joe has never liked me. Perhaps in some way it is my fault and Mother is right," Aine said, feeling defeated that she had to agree with her mother for once.

"I don't think your mother is right, by the way. That did not give Joe the right to act out the way he did towards either you or your sister. I have known your mother for a long time, Aine, and she always sides with wrong choices. Apart from your father, who should have stood up to her a long, long time ago. But that last bit has nothing to do with this and is just my opinion," Detective Hampton said. He got up and walked to the door. "Come on, let's see if the doctors have any news. Plus, I need to see if the security cameras will give anything else." Aine got up and followed him down the corridor the way they had come back to Anchorette's room.

Dr. Sullivan was just leaving the room when Aine and the detective approached him. "How are Anchorette and the baby doing?" Aine asked, hastily trying to see past his shoulder as he closed the door.

"She is doing well and so is her baby," Dr. Sullivan assured her. "She is just resting up. You can go in and see her once the nurses have finished attending to her."

"Dr. Sullivan, I am Detective Hampton. Could I ask you some questions if you have a few minutes? I would also like to ask questions to your staff, and request security to locate the film for the camera on this ward."

"Of course, this way. Aine, you may go in, but please don't tire Anchorette out. She needs to rest," Dr. Sullivan said. "Detective, if you would like to follow me?" This time the doctor led the detective away.

Chapter Twenty-Two

Aine

Aine closed the door to Anchorette's room. The two policemen had been standing outside since she had entered. There was no sign of Detective Hampton. Anchorette had been given a sedative to help her calm down, so Aine knew there was no point in hanging around. She needed to get the bus back to the house and was still figuring out the bus routes and the quickest way.

She walked out of the hospital, avoiding all the shadows and spirits that were roaming around aimlessly. Sometimes they wanted to talk to her, but Aine just didn't have it in her to give the care or hope that they were looking for.

Her stomach growled at her, a reminder that she hadn't eaten since the day before. There was a bakery on her way to the bus stop, and she stopped to pick up some muffins and a morning cup of strong coffee.

The bus was a little crowded with people going into work or doing their morning shopping. A spirit stood on the bus wearing his conductor's outfit, shouting, "Tickets, please." He was standing close to the passengers, who were not aware of his presence. Aine took her phone out of her coat pocket and unwrapped some earphones. Plugging them in, she turned on her music and closed her eyes, hoping the spirit would stay down at the front end of the bus. As the journey went on more people got off, and eventually there was only one person besides herself on board, a woman sitting up front. The spirit was now sitting in front of Aine. She switched off her music, took out the earbuds, and took a sip of her coffee now that it was cooler. The conductor turned around to look at her.

"You blind woman. You're not allowed to drink or eat hot food on the buses." He pointed to the sign up at the front.

"Sorry," Aine said quietly, putting the coffee back down next to the muffins.

The conductor blinked and looked at her. "Wait, you can see me?" he asked.

"For my sins it would appear so," Aine replied. She wanted to get off of the bus, but she was a good two miles away from town and was still sore from sleeping in the hospital the night before.

"I can't remember the last time someone actually spoke to me. It must have been at least a decade ago if not more," the conductor said.

"You are aware that you are a spirit and should have moved along into the otherworld?" Aine asked him quietly.

The conductor nodded knowingly and looked away. "I moved away from the mist and it has not come back since," he said. "Are you here to help me?" he asked hopefully.

Aine was not sure if she was here to help him or not. "I honestly don't know," she replied.

"You've not done this before, have you?" he asked, a little hurt.

"No, this is all new to me and I'm not sure how to handle it. But I can put in a word for you, as my grandmama and aunt sometimes see me. Next time I speak to them I can ask them to help you out," Aine said, starting to feel sorry for him.

The bus conductor got up and walked away to the front of the bus. He sat close to the driver. Aine sat for the rest of the journey wondering what it must be like to be stuck here in this world with no way out. The bus conductor had not said anything else, and Aine's journey on the bus was coming to an end. She got her stuff together, and as she walked past the conductor she stopped and looked down at him.

"I won't forget to ask," she whispered to him.

The bus stopped, and as she got off she heard him speak as the doors closed. "Thank you." The bus drove off with the conductor sitting at the back and waving at Aine as she watched the bus travel on its journey.

Aine turned once the bus had gone out of sight and set off down the road back to where it had all started.

Chapter Twenty-Three

Aine

It seemed odd entering the house where Joe had attacked. Aine had grabbed Anchorette's keys when the police took her to the hospital less than week ago now. Anchorette had left the keys in the front door when she entered the house that morning. Aine put the keys on the kitchen counter and grabbed a plate to put a muffin on. Next she grabbed a coffee mug and poured the now cool coffee into it.

Minstral meowed and Midnight and Guinness followed in a chorus.

"Sorry, guys. I know you haven't been fed for a while now," Aine said, feeling really guilty.

She looked through the cupboard and found tins of cat food stacked up next to an opened bag of biscuits. Guinness jumped up and onto the counter, impatient for food, as Aine poured the biscuits onto three clean plates and then searched for the tin opener in the draws.

As she scooped the food out of the tins she decided a quick shower was in order.

"Okay, guys, I shall be back shortly," Aine said, putting the plates down on the floor. Going up the stairs felt odd, and being alone in the house was really creepy.

The shower was short and sweet. As Aine got dressed she wondered what clothes to take in for Anchorette. Obviously nightshirts were a must, as was a wash bag. Going back down the stairs, Aine muttered to herself the items required. She headed towards the kitchen to make a list as she waited for Grandmama and Aunt Hettie.

She didn't remember the back door being open.

A shadow formed in the door frame, and a woman came into view. It was one of the nurses from the attack on Anchorette. Looking closer at her, Aine finally managed to place the face, realizing where she had seen her all those years ago. "Lindsey? What are you doing here?" Aine asked, not liking it one bit.

"Well, I thought I would finish off what I started this morning," Lindsey said, taking a knife out from behind her back. Aine raised her eyebrow, not sure if it was real.

"Um, this is slightly odd. Why are you planning to put a knife in me?" Aine asked, trying to think a way out of the situation.

"Did you really think that Joe and I would end our relationship just because you threatened to tell Anchorette?" Lindsey spat out her question while taking a step into the house. Aine took a step back.

"Well, most with a conscience would," Aine said, realizing that her quick line there was not a good idea.

"It didn't take much to get rid of you, though. Just offer you some good-quality drugs and you were gone, forgetting all about Anchorette and Joe. It didn't take much to get Brett's family to get you hooked and messed up. Shame you didn't take up Joe's offer a few days ago," Lindsey said.

"Wait, you're telling me that you and Joe have been seeing each other all this time? I thought you were Anchorette's friend. Even in high school you two were friends," Aine said, confused.

"We were never friends. I was assigned to become her friend," Lindsey said angrily.

"You were assigned? By the dark shadow slayers?" Aine asked.

"Well done. Yes, I was assigned when I was in my teens to become friends with Anchorette. Then gradually I would introduce her to some of my male friends. Joe was originally assigned to you. But we soon noticed that you were ruining your own future, and so one less person for us to concern ourselves with.

"Joe was grateful when our commander dropped you and he was assigned to Anchorette. It made it so much easier for us to stay together all these years. That was up till you decided to try and split us up. Joe has only ever loved me. We will be together and we will be taking Keith and that unborn child," Lindsey said, inching closer.

"You've got some issues in the maternal section, and somehow I can't see Anchorette agreeing with you," Aine said.

"She won't get much of a say after the baby is born and Anchorette is no longer breathing and is dead," Lindsey said with a grin.

Aine didn't know what to say or do.

"Okay, so you intend to kill me, wait till Anchorette has given birth, and then go play happy family with Joe, who is locked up for trying to murder Anchorette and give me a fatal drug overdose," Aine said, knowing she was running out of time to stall Lindsey.

"Sounds about right," Lindsey agreed.

It was at this point that the doorbell rang and the letter box rattled.

"I wouldn't make a sound. If you do, I will kill you," Lindsey warned.

"Aine, this is Detective Hampton. Are you home?"

Aine relieved, shouted, "Help me, I'm in here."

"You little bitch," Lindsey sneered. She went to Aine with her arm outstretched. The knife tore through Aine's t-shirt as she ran to the front door and tried to open it. She screamed as cold metal scraped at her back again.

The front door banged three times, and as Aine fell to the floor the detective burst through the front door with his gun out. "Stop or I will shoot," Detective Hampton shouted as he spotted Lindsey kneeling on top of Aine with a knife to her throat.

"I said stop or I will shoot," Detective Hampton said, stepping closer towards them.

"This isn't over," Lindsey said, putting the knife down and putting her hands up.

"Why does that not surprise me?" Aine muttered.

Chapter Twenty-Four

Aine

"So what happens now?" Aine asked Detective Hampton as Lindsey was escorted out by two police officers.

It hadn't taken Detective Hampton long to realize that Aine had gone back to the house. After reading through Aine's statement, he knew there was a possibility that the attackers would try to hurt Aine back at the house, so he had gone there to make sure she was okay.

"She won't make bail, and with the statement you just gave me I'm guessing both she and Joe will be sentenced for a very long time. Joe has been very uncooperative at the station and has not said a single word. I just don't get it. Why would Joe and Lindsey do this to Anchorette?" Detective Hampton wondered.

"It is a mystery," Aine agreed. Of course when she had given her latest statement she had not mentioned the society of dark shadow slayers. Aine had thought fast on that one. With Lindsey having been sleeping with Joe all those years, and with what Lindsey had said in the kitchen just then, the lie came to her fluently.

"What about Keith? You know she had another person helping her, so he isn't safe right now. Surely social services will let me have access to him?" Aine asked in hope.

"It will be noted that you, Anchorette, and Keith need to be placed under protection and that in the best interest for Keith you should be with him. But it would also strengthen your case if you did some rehab counselling and helped us with Mr. Brett Hunter's family," Detective Hampton said more seriously.

"I know. My memory is coming back to me, but some of it is just not as clear as it should be and I'm trying real hard to remember it all. Can I come down to the station tomorrow after I have been to the hospital to check up on Anchorette?" Aine asked, hoping to buy herself some extra time. She really needed to speak with Grandmama and Aunt Hettie, but with all that had gone on she suspected they had stayed away.

"Yes, I suppose I can allow you this. But you must show up tomorrow, Aine, given the circumstances. We can't delay our investigation for much longer, or it will all slip through our fingers."

Aine nodded and smiled, a little relieved. The wound to her back was superficial and didn't require stitches, just a large plaster. The top of Aine's back was covered mostly with large padding and would now need a large plaster. She felt awful at how it would all look. Nothing compared to how Anchorette's would be. Tears flooded her eyes again at the thought of Anchorette suffering not just physically but emotionally. For all those years her marriage had been a sham, and all along Aine knew that Joe had been having an affair. She had known about the society but she had never listened to either Grandmama or Aunt Hettie. Oh, how she wished she had now. The guilt was eating away at her, but she knew she had no right to feel sorry for herself. The tiny cough that came from Detective Hampton broke Aine out of her feeling of guilt.

"We're ready to leave, if you will be all right on your own," he said.

Aine wiped her eyes. "Um, yep, I'm okay. I shall see you tomorrow then," Aine said, trying to keep her voice from wobbling.

Detective Hampton could see she was putting on a brave face but that she wanted some privacy. He nodded. "Okay, then. I shall see you tomorrow," he said, and with that Aine was left alone with the sound of the front door closing.

Aine sat on the sofa, sobbing. Her eyes were swelling up, and she didn't want to be alone. She headed to the kitchen where the cats had been placed earlier by the police officer.

Chapter Twenty-Five

Grandmama Hartwood

" That girl needs to toughen up more. She is a Hartwood and we need to be strong," Grandmama said to her daughter Hettie.

"Mother, give the girl a break. In case you haven't noticed, she has been through the mill, and it is not like we gave her a chance to get used to it as a child and teen, either," Aunt Hettie said, trying to keep her voice low. She knew that her mother was right, but she also remembered what it was like to be a teen and how it had affected her sister Janet. They could both hear Aine crying in the front room and had stayed away just in case there were any other dark shadow slayers in the area. But with the police still in the area they were safe for now.

"Do you think one of us should go see if she needs anything?"

"Like what?" Grandmama snapped. "It's not like we can cuddle her, you know, or make her a cupper." One of the chairs tucked in around the dining room table came out at the flick of her wrist. She sat down and waited.

"I know you're feeling as guilty as I am for leaving the girls alone when they were younger. But you remember how Janet was, especially towards Aine," Hettie said, coming closer to her mother.

"Don't presume to tell me how I feel, Hettie, and especially not about Janet. We abided by her wishes and now we are the ones being punished for it. If we do not get to that—" Grandmama Hartwood didn't finish her sentence, as just then Aine walked in with tears running down her face.

"Oh." Aine stopped, wiping her tears away hastily.

"Aine, how are you?" Grandmama Hartwood asked, standing up from the chair. She clasped her hands together. Aunt Hettie could see the frustration in her face at how much she wanted to touch Aine but couldn't. She did feel guilty, just as much as Hettie did.

"I don't have much time to talk right now. I need to get to Anchorette and grab clothing for myself. I can't come back here."

"You need to put the kettle on and get some food into you. Then we can talk," Grandmama Hartwood said.

The kettle started to boil and Aine looked at Grandmama Hartwood. "Okay, but I really do not have much time," Aine said.

Grandmama Hartwood smiled and nodded. "We know, child," she replied.

The coffee felt good, and so did the blueberry muffin. Aine swallowed her last mouthful and breathed in a little deeply. Aunt Hettie and Grandmama had joined her at the dining room table and were seated on either side of her.

"Okay," Aine said, looking down with a slow nod of recognition. "Right, time to get a move on." She readied herself to stand up and focus.

"Not just yet, Aine. We need your help a little, and we have answers for you as far as Brett goes," Aunt Hettie said.

That knocked Aine down a little. She had forgotten about Brett but knew she would have to get those answers before Detective Hampton came back asking for more.

"Okay," Aine said.

"We need you to keep with the plan of moving to Canada. The detective will place all of you into protective police custody for the time being. He will be stubborn about you all moving to Canada and will need persuading, but you must stick with the plan, Aine. A lot of things weigh heavily on all the choices and steps that are made. As you know, we cannot tell you much about the other side. But some heavy things are happening. We need help from this side to prevent it as much as possible. Everyone's future is in danger," Aunt Hettie said. She looked at her mother.

"Do you think you can help us to do this, Aine?" Grandmama Hartwood asked.

"I can try. I think the detective might listen to me now, as he needs information about Brett's family. So if I can make a deal with him he should agree to it," Aine said.

"Ah yes, Mr. Hunter, we have spoken to him. Aine, he wanted to take the opportunity to speak to you. We were not sure of how you would react to him being here," Grandmama Hartwood said.

"I would have liked to have spoken to him," Aine said in a hopeful tone.

"You must remember and know this Aine: we can only allow you to see Brett once. He has committed crimes in this world that have to be answered for in our world," Grandmama Hartwood said sternly.

"I know, I just would like to speak to him one last time, please," Aine said. Grandmama Hartwood closed her eyes and nodded.

In front of Aine the wall began to shimmer, and then an outline of three figures walking towards her appeared. Brett stood in front of her. He looked just as she remembered him. He was wearing black jeans and a checked black-and-white shirt. Wrapped around his wrists were glowing gold cords. Behind him stood a man and a woman dressed in black trousers and white shirts. They didn't say anything, they just stood behind Brett.

The empty chair in front of Aine moved out and Brett sat down.

"Hey, Aine," Brett said cheerfully. "You've been busy, I hear."

Aine sat looking at Brett. Her breathing became rapid.

"I don't have much time, Brett. I need you to tell me about your family and the drugs. I need answers and anything else you can tell me. Please, Brett." Aine was hurting and she knew she would lose it soon.

"Sure, babe, you know I will tell you what I can," Brett said, smiling.

"You didn't tell me all when you were alive, Brett," Aine said, feeling hurt.

"Neither did you, it would appear," Brett replied. Aine saw the hurt in his eyes. She had kept her talent a secret from him.

"Well, guess we are now equal. You know my secret, Brett, but if I had not had this little secret, I would have been set up and blamed for crimes that you and your brother did," Aine said. She was hurting, all right. Betrayal and loss were battling in her head and making it ache.

"Enough. Answer her questions, Brett," Grandmama Hartwood snapped at him.

"Aine, firstly I wanted to let you know that I wouldn't have done what I did if I hadn't been on the drugs. I know this to be true. I would have loved you every inch that I did. But as you know, my brother is a mean bastard. He was approached one evening by a very persuasive woman who told him to get you hooked on drugs. I did at first try to stop him, and you as well. But you wouldn't listen to me. You listened to my brother more. To sweeten you even more, he insisted that we go travelling. He would send drugs to me to sell in other countries, but he didn't tell me where he had gotten them from. I spied on him one evening when he met up with some man named Mr. Miller."

Aine gasped in realization: Anchorette's marital name was Miller.

"I didn't know that there was any connection until I was brought to the other world. I was asked questions and finally introduced to your grandmama and your aunt Hettie," Brett finished.

"Be careful, Brett," Grandmama Hartwood said.

Aine looked from Grandmama Hartwood to Brett and then to Aunt Hettie. She looked back at Brett. The gold cords around his wrists started to glow brighter.

"What are those things around your wrists, Brett?" Aine asked.

"That is not of your concern, Aine. What is of your concern is that you now need to let the police know all the information Brett has given you," Grandmama Hartwood said before Brett could say anything else. Grandmama Hartwood looked at Brett.

"Your grandmama is correct. I spied that night and overheard Mr. Miller asking how well the business was raising money. It was for another project but I didn't get to hear about that, as Mr. Miller didn't talk about it. He wanted to know about you and if you were still alive. That angered me a lot, and that was when he and my brother heard me. I was beaten for hours, Aine, in a warehouse that is close to the dive. You remember the pool hall we went to a few years ago." Brett looked into Aine's eyes. She nodded. "I was thrown in the back of the car and driven back to where you were sleeping. I wasn't conscious much, and my brother loaded a syringe and gave me the drug overdose. I tried to tell you to leave." Brett's voice broke.

"I remember you telling me to leave. I remember your body laying there and not moving. I didn't want to leave you, Brett, but you told me to," Aine said, trying hard not to cry. "I'm so sorry, this is all my fault," Aine said, starting to sob.

"It is not your fault, Aine, it is a path that none of us chose. If we could all change our deaths, we would. We can't change our paths, but you can change yours," Aunt Hettie said.

"What happens now?" Aine asked, looking at Brett.

"You change your path and live. You stop whatever is coming our way," Brett said.

"You also help others and your sister," Grandmama Hartwood said.

Aine sat crying for a little while longer.

"Time to go," Grandmama Hartwood said to Brett.

"No, you can't let him go yet. I have one more question to ask him," Aine said, pulling herself together. "Those gold cords on your wrists, are you under arrest somehow? If there is a trial and it has to do with me, then I forgive him. It was not his fault," Aine said.

"As noble as this all is, Aine, and while you're not far off the mark, Brett did cause many deaths due to the drugs that were sold," Aunt Hettie said.

"Yes, but at the hand of his brother. I know what he is like. It is not all his fault," Aine said firmly.

One of the gold cords shimmered on his wrist. His left wrist was now clear.

"Thank you." Brett smiled gratefully.

"It would appear you were heard. But, Aine, you have other things to focus on," Grandmama Hartwood said.

"Yes, yes, you are correct. I have something to ask you, Grandmama, but not right now." She looked at Brett, knowing it would be a long while before she saw him again. "Brett, I'm sorry this happened to us. Please don't forget me." Aine hiccupped, trying so hard not to cry again. "I wish we could have had more time together," Aine said, trying to smile through her tears.

"Hey, just because you can't see me doesn't mean that I'm not looking in. You just focus on the task in front of you, girl, and keep your head down low. It is all good, Aine, and we are all here for you. You and your sister will be all right," Brett said, getting up from his seat. He turned towards the two people who had been standing right behind him the whole time.

"Be good, behave, and stay strong, Aine," Brett said as he faded into the shimmering wall he had appeared from.

"Please Grandmama, Aunt Hettie, look after him." Aine sobbed into a never-ending pile of tissues.

"We are doing our best, Aine, and the people who count in our world have heard you," Aunt Hettie answered.

"Grandmama, on the way here there was a man on the bus I was travelling on. He was stuck there and asked me to help him, but I didn't know what to do. Do you think you could help him?" Aine asked, looking at her.

"Ah, you mean Phil. You can only guide him to the light. It is the spirit's choice to leave when he is ready. The spirit itself calls forth the light and is guided from either this side or the other. If he had been ready he would have already called for it." Grandmama Hartwood placed her hand over her heart. She smiled warmly.

"We can't help them all. Only the ones who are seeking it," Aunt Hettie said.

"Now you, my girl, need to go upstairs and get your and Anchorette's things together, as well as Keith's. And you need to find a place for the cats," Grandmama Hartwood said.

"What will I do with the cats?" Aine panicked: she hadn't thought about that.

"The neighbour seems to be lonely and rather fond of them. Perhaps you could ask her to help you out until you are all settled and ready over in Canada?" Aunt Hettie suggested.

Aine nodded, trusting their advice. She went upstairs and packed things of need and importance, leaving Grandmama Hartwood and Aunt Hettie alone.

"Well, that went better than expected," Grandmama Hartwood said to her daughter.

"Do you think Brett stands a chance, or do you think they will imprison him for all eternity? You know that the people he wronged might not be as forgiving," Aunt Hettie said.

"I know, and it might be best regardless of the outcome if we tell Aine that it all went well. But we should perhaps go to the hearing and lend our support to Brett," Grandmama Hartwood said as she faded out of the dining room.

Chapter Twenty-Six

Aine

Aine came back down to find that she was alone in the house.

She had packed as many of her things as she could in such a short time, but it wasn't hard, as she had come here with very little. Most of Keith's items had already been removed. Social services must have come in and taken them, along with his toys and clothing. It was difficult to assess what Anchorette would and would not want, so Aine packed a mixture of tops and jumpers along with skirts and jeans. Next she took what little jewellery was in her box. Even if Anchorette didn't want to keep the jewellery, she could sell it or put it to one side till she had decided.

She took the suitcase downstairs and left it close to the front door next to a small holder bag.

Next, the cats. Somehow Aine felt hurt about having left them behind, and she was sure they had felt the same. "Sounds silly, you know, but I can't help but wonder if you guys were here protecting my sister and nephew as best as you could," Aine said as Minstral came up and rubbed himself against her leg.

Aine bent down to stroke him. "I'm going to do my best to get you and Midnight and Guinness to wherever it is we end up. But for now Grandmama has suggested the lady across the street," Aine said, getting up and walking to the front door. Minstral meowed as she closed it, bringing Aine to tears again.

Once she had composed herself she spoke to the nice lady across the street, who agreed to take on Anchorette's cats and was eager to receive some gossip as to what had happened. Aine of course was careful not to give out too much information.

She went back across the street to grab the cats. Sitting in his car outside the front door was Detective Hampton. He got out as he saw Aine approach.

"Aine, we need to hurry up, please. Some disturbing news has come to light," Detective Hampton said as he met her at the front door.

"Why, what's happened?" Aine asked, unlocking the front door.

"Good, you're all packed." He grabbed the large suitcase and the small holder bag. "If there is anything else, then please hurry and grab it while I load up," he said, walking back to the car.

Aine looked around quickly. She saw the other muffin and picked it up on her way out. She locked the front door and walked to the car. Detective Hampton raised an eyebrow at seeing the muffin.

"I have not had the chance to eat much," Aine said, defending herself.

"Come on, hurry please," the detective said, getting into his car.

Aine followed round to the other side. She got in and did her seat belt up. The detective started the car and they drove out onto the street where it had all begun.

"What news came through?" Aine asked, picking at her cherry muffin.

"The social service contacted us and told us that a woman claiming to be you had tried to take Keith. Of course the social worker who was working at that time has had the unfortunate pleasure of meeting you—her words, not mine, may I add—and so knew something was not right. The police were contacted and I came here. Keith is being transferred to a safe house. This of course means that both you and he will be placed together under protective custody, and I'm sorry to say, no more visits to see Anchorette." Aine opened her mouth to protest, but she didn't get a chance. "This is not open to discussion, Aine. We need to keep all three of you safe. Anchorette is under constant police surveillance. You have to focus on Keith now, as she will be worrying about him. We will set up daily phone calls for you so that she can be at ease." The detective finished and waited for Aine to respond. She sat in silence for a while.

"Do you think it was possibly the other woman from the hospital this morning?" Aine asked. She knew it had to be, or at least someone from the society keen to get Keith into the camp. But she couldn't mention that to the detective.

"We believe so, but again, she ran off before police arrived to arrest her. Do you know what is going on here?" Detective Hampton asked.

"I'm not sure, but my memory is getting clearer as far as Brett's family goes," Aine supplied, hoping he would see the catch coming. He nodded.

"Well, that is good, Aine, but first up let's get you to the safe house," Detective Hampton said. He relaxed a little; Aine was going to give him something he could work with.

Chapter Twenty-Seven

Joe

B eing in a prison was no different to growing up in a training camp. If you followed the rules and did what was asked of you and kept to yourself, then trouble would not come knocking on your door.

Joe soon knew that the last bit was not as true as people who were easily fooled would believe. Unfortunately in a prison even trouble could still leak through the system. When Joe received a request for visitation, he knew he had two options: either allow the visitor in, or wait for the visitor to do damage from outside.

He sat in the hall with the other inmates wearing a bright red bib vest. The bars, he noticed, were slimmer than the ones in the training camps he had grown up in. In those camps, escape meant an immediate death sentence. He remembered quite a few friends along the way disappearing. No one asked about them, as they all knew what the answer would be.

He rested his arms on the table and waited as the guards opened a barred iron door. Families and friends filed through to see their loved ones. Some were emotional; some were angry. Eventually Joe's visitor came through and he stood up greet him. The visitor's face was composed and seemed calm, but his eyes told Joe that he was not calm or composed at all.

Joe swallowed hard as his friend Martin walked towards him and sat in the empty seat across from him.

"Hello," Joe said.

Martin nodded his head.

"I didn't expect to see you so soon, but thank you for coming," Joe said quietly. His friend waited to respond, as a guard was walking past.

"Well, as your representative in this case I felt it was wise to come here and get as much of the facts as I could before we stand trial. There are a lot of questions that need to be answered. Firstly, how you could have let this happen?"

Martin had come there pretending to be Joe's solicitor, but he knew that Joe was not the only one who was going to stand trial. Their commander would have spoken to Joe's father to find out what had gone wrong. Their commander would have made it clear that Joe's failure reflected on his father and was punishable by death. Martin was the go-between sent by Joe's father.

"I followed the plan that was discussed the night before. Anchorette had left the house to go out. So while Keith was still sleeping I got up and went to the bathroom. I could hear Aine making noises, so I went inside to see. The drugs were laid out and I went to take them away from her. As I left with them she attacked me, so I defended myself. I tied her to the bed. I was just about to leave when Anchorette came back. Having seen me tying her sister to the bed, she went at me hysterically. I think seeing me with the drugs in my hands did not help." Joe saw that Martin understood what he really meant. Joe had gone into the bedroom while Anchorette was out and Aine was sleeping. But when Joe was about inject Aine, she somehow woke up and fought him off. Then Anchorette came back and walked in seeing Joe trying to inject Aine while she was tied up.

"I panicked, and Anchorette was not waking up. I didn't know what to do, so I put her in the car and drove."

Martin knew where he would have been driving to. With the extensive injuries he had inflicted on her in his rage, he would have been taking Anchorette to the seer and her sister, a healing sage.

"So Anchorette left the car how?" Martin asked.

Joe cleared his throat. "I was not focusing straight. She must have come to, and thinking I was going to kill her, she tried to jump out of the car. I lost concentration on my driving. I didn't know the lorry in front had braked. We crashed. The next thing I knew Anchorette was in the ambulance and I was just coming to," Joe said.

"I shall have to go back and speak to my boss to see how we can help get you free," Martin said, looking at Joe.

"What about my son Keith? Is he safe?" Joe asked.

"We are doing everything we can to gain access to him, but social services are proving to be difficult." This was not the answer Joe was hoping for. Keith should have been at the commander's centre by now. Martin got up with the briefcase he had carried in. Joe recognized it for what it really was. Martin had been recording the whole conversation.

"Thank you for giving me a chance to put my side across," Joe said.

He watched as Martin left. He didn't know where he stood. Martin said he would try to get him free, but how? Would the commander let him go free? Joe shook his head, knowing the answer to that last one. No one was free, not when you were born a dark shadow slayer. You either accepted it or were put to death. It was a choice you made on your first day of adulthood.

When Joe turned eighteen, he had already decided to accept that his heart followed Lindsey, even though they had been in training to seek out the abomination and set up homes with them. Some of them passed that test easily. They would be set small tasks like slipping them a drug to suppress their talents. They would court and woo them so that they believed every single lie they were told. They would set up a family home with them and impregnate them so their children could be used and harnessed against them all. They were also trained to kill if they were ever found out.

Joe was sure that Aine knew who and what he was. The cameras set up around the house and in her bedroom confirmed his suspicions when he went back to Martin's flat. Martin, of course, had been watching her from a distance. But the day Martin heard Aine and Anchorette talking about moving and taking Keith, he had phoned Joe to talk about taking Aine out permanently. Lindsey and her cousin Lacey had both been there as well. They planned it all out that day and evening. But somehow something had gone wrong and Aine had woken up before Joe could inject her with the lethal dose of heroin. It would have gone perfectly well, but now nothing made any sense.

"Time, please," one of the guards shouted. The prisoners hugged their loved ones, and the loved ones cried as they left. *I would give anything to hug my Lindsey right now, just to smell her and breathe all of her in.*

Chapter Twenty-Eight

Joe

It had hurt Joe to see Martin treat him as a common criminal. He stood in line waiting his turn to use the phone. It was difficult for him to keep his temper under control, but he had to find out why Janet had not at least tried to gain access to Keith. It just didn't make any sense that she hadn't.

Finally it was his turn. He dialled the number and waited. Finally, an answer.

"Hello?" His luck was in: it was Janet.

"Hello, Janet, it is Joe here. How are you?" He wasn't sure as to how she would be now. If Aine had poisoned her against him, he wouldn't get anywhere at all.

"I'm doing good, Joe, but should you be calling me?" Janet sounded shaky. Perhaps it was nerves, but he had to press on.

"It's okay, Janet, I just need to know how Keith is doing."

"Keith, from what I have been told, is doing well. Social services won't allow me any access due to Anchorette's say-so." Janet was crying.

"Anchorette won't allow you? That is silly, Janet. Have you tried to talk to her since we last spoke?" Joe was infuriated that Anchorette had denied her mother access. He knew what it was like to not have a mother in his life. It was one of the reasons why he cherished Lindsey so much.

"Joe, I did speak to her. But I think Aine is influencing her somehow. Joe, she told me she was pregnant again."

He stood there in silence. *What have I done to her?* His breathing became shaky.

"Joe, are you there? Did you hear me?" Janet asked.

"Um, yeah—sorry. You're sure?" He had to be sure. If she was, then he would need to get offline and let his father know immediately.

"Yes, she told me on the phone. I don't think she meant to, as she was very angry with me, Joe. She didn't like that I had spoken to you before."

"That's okay, Janet. You should probably not let her know that we have spoken this time," Joe said.

"She is refusing my calls to the hospital, so I couldn't speak to her even if I wanted to, Joe. I just don't know how this all happened," Janet said, sobbing.

"I'm sorry, Janet, I have to go now. The person behind me needs to use the phone. Bye, Janet." He hung up before she could sob her pitiful self down the line any further. He put the receiver back up and punched in the next number.

"Hey, it's my turn." Joe turned to see the prisoner in line behind him getting hot in the cheeks.

"Just give me a second to leave a message, and then you'll get your turn." Joe looked him right in the eye. It was that or he wouldn't get a call at all. Joe's right hand was wrapped around the phone cord, ready to pull and use as a strangling tool. The other prisoner saw it and backed off.

"Hello?" It was Martin who answered.

"Martin, tell father Anchorette is pregnant again. I have to go." Joe hung up. "See, that was difficult," he said as he walked past.

Chapter Twenty-Nine

Mr. Miller

"Well?" Mr. Miller asked Martin.

Mr. Miller pulled out of the prison car park. He hated leaving Joe locked up, but the decision was out of his hands.

"You know I cannot tell you what was said, but I do believe he was out numbered," Martin said. "I'm sorry, I know this is not what you would like to hear, but I still have evidence that I need to put forward."

"Did Joe ask about Keith or the sisters?" Mr. Miller asked, changing the topic. He knew that Martin was right. Mr. Miller had grown up with Martin's father in the camps and had been firm friends with him until he was killed by an Irish family. Mr. Miller had taken Martin on as one of his own. A family disappearing was something you got used to growing up where they did.

"He asked about Keith but only talked about the sisters to explain what had happened. I told him that Keith was with social services. Is that still the situation now?" Martin asked.

"Unfortunately yes, for the time being. Lacey tried to gain access to Keith by pretending to be Aine, but social services did not believe her and so she left before the police arrived. Of course it does not help that she has not been focused since Lindsey was arrested late this morning. It would appear that all our plans are falling to the wayside except for one. The brooch I gave to Anchorette as a wedding present has been moved. It is heading northwest, out of the city," Mr. Miller said, looking for a second or two at Martin.

"Well, at least that is something. We shall have to hold another meeting to see what the commander says," Martin said.

"Yes, it is a little relieving to know that we can go back with some good news of sorts," Mr. Miller said, driving to the motorway that would take them back to camp.

The phone rang. Mr. Miller reached over and looked at the number but didn't recognize it. He passed it to Martin.

"Hello?" Martin answered.

Martin put the phone to his ear but didn't say anything. After a moment he hung up.

"Who was it?" Mr. Miller asked.

"That was Joe. He said Anchorette is pregnant again."

"Well, that changes the goalpost a little bit, doesn't it?" Mr. Miller slowed down to have a little more time to process the thought. The rest of the drive passed in silence.

Chapter Thirty

Aine

Aine was exhausted. The car journey had been long and had taken them to a house on the outskirts of what looked like a nice town.

Detective Hampton was in the dining room making a few calls. Aine overheard him talking to a social worker, who was clearly not at all comfortable with the idea of returning Keith to her.

"I'm telling you to bring that child here. I have known Aine since she was a child and I have also known Keith's grandmother since we were kids in the playground. Now would you please not try to go up against me?" Detective Hampton hung up and put his phone in his trouser pocket. He pulled out a handkerchief: he was sweating. With the pressure of his job and now dealing with protective custody and policemen on guard at the hospital, he was stretching himself. His age didn't help, either.

"Thank you," Aine said, coming into full view from behind the door. "I should have realized my mother would voice her concerns about me looking after Keith," Aine said, taking one of the seats at the table.

"Yes, your mother has been voicing her opinion, and while I might a while back have agreed with her, I have now seen how you have changed. Do you mind?" Detective Hampton asked, pointing to an empty seat.

"No, please," Aine said. "I know you have seen me grow up a rebel, but I also know where to draw the line. But the same cannot be said for Brett's family. What they did to him was unforgivable. I will tell you everything I know and can remember, Detective, but you must promise me that you will help me, Anchorette, and Keith set up a new life outside of this country. I know you are under a lot of pressure, but we will be in great danger if we stay here," Aine said, laying her cards out and knowing it might tip the scale, not necessarily in her favour.

Detective Hampton sat, took his handkerchief out, and wiped his brow. "I can't make you any promises here, Aine, but I know how big this is for you and Anchorette," he said. Aine could see his mind weighing the options and whether it would be possible. "You are going to have to give me time to speak to my boss. I can't make any guarantees here. But you know you will have to give evidence and that you will be held in contempt of court if you do not," Detective Hampton finished. He looked right into Aine's eyes.

She knew this. The pressure they were both under was a ticking time bomb, with Aine trying to keep the scales evenly balanced out. She knew he was under strain as it was, but she was under a lot of strain as well. Her grandmama and aunt had not told her what was going on, but it was obvious that they wanted her and Anchorette to leave the country. Perhaps they knew something about their destinies and didn't want either of them to die to early.

Aine nodded, looking right back at Detective Hampton. She knew she had to gamble here. It was now time to see how well-balanced the scales were.

"Okay, Detective, get your pen and paper out. Hope you don't get writer's cramp," Aine said.

Detective Hampton smiled, a little tired. He got up and went to the kitchen counter, where his coat had been resting. From one of his pockets he pulled out a small recording machine.

"If you don't mind, I think this is a little more reliable compared to my handwriting and my ability to keep up with people's thoughts," he answered, sitting back down and placing the device on the table. He pressed the button and it started recording. Aine knew it would be a long night. But she also knew that the sooner it was done, the sooner she could push for Canada.

After Detective Hampton wrapped up the interview, the social worker arrived with Keith. Aine was overjoyed. The social worker was not as happy to see Aine, but Aine did not care for her thoughts. Keith was happy to see Aine— it was clear he was happy to see a face he recognized—but he kept looking around for his mother. It saddened Aine that Keith didn't understand. True to Detective Hampton's words, he had set up a system for Anchorette to place a call to the house. Aine was so relieved to hear Anchorette's voice.

"Hello, Anchorette, are you all right? I couldn't believe what happened this morning," Aine said emotionally over the phone. Keith, wriggling in her arms, tried to grab the phone from her. He screamed in frustration.

"I'm okay, but how is Keith? Is he okay?" Anchorette was eager to know that Keith was okay, and Aine couldn't blame her. "Can you bring him to me at the hospital, please? I miss him so much, Aine," Anchorette pleaded down the phone.

"Anchorette, I can't. I am in a safe house with him. The social worker is not happy with me having him here, and plus Detective Hampton would pitch a fit. You need to concentrate on getting well, and soon. I gave my statement to Detective Hampton, and he is doing his job investigating as we speak. It would be dangerous right now if I left here with Keith, and you know I am right," Aine said, hurting inside.

"Do you know what happened to me this morning?" Anchorette asked.

"Yes, I know what happened. Detective Hampton has placed security outside your door. I intend to have words with—well, you know what with, and keep you as safe as I can," Aine said. "I never knew Lindsey was this delusional, Anchorette, and if I had known then I would have said something well before."

"It was Lindsey who did this to me, but why?" Anchorette asked tearfully.

"I don't know the whys, Anchorette, all I know is that it was her, and another woman was with her. She looked similar to her, and I have a feeling it has something to do with what I was talking to you about a few nights back. But I just don't know how it is all connected yet," Aine said.

"Okay. I am being told time by the nurse guarding the phone, so I shall speak to you tomorrow. Tell Keith that Mummy loves him and will be with him soon," Anchorette said with tears in her voice before the line went dead.

"I will," Aine said to the silence.

Chapter Thirty-One

Aine

"You all set?" Detective Hampton asked as Aine kissed Keith good-bye.

Aine nodded shakily. The months of hiding had been stressful. Anchorette was due to leave the hospital today and they would all be relocated to another safe house after Aine had given her testimony. Anchorette had had a successful operation to fix her intestines and repair other minor injuries. The baby was fine and unharmed, much to Aine's relief. The trial for Brett Hunter had been taking place in court for the past week, and everyone in the house was tense. More security guards had been added around the house, as Aine was due to give her evidence in court. Some guards would be going with her and Detective Hampton, while others would stay behind to protect Keith and the social worker who had come to take their belongings to the new location. Joe's family, whoever they were, had not stopped trying to gain access to Anchorette and Keith. Anchorette had told Aine some alarming things in their nightly phone calls. Anchorette had been moved to two different hospitals within the city, but they had somehow managed to find out where she was. It didn't make sense how they knew where she was; Aunt Hettie let Aine know a few nights before that she didn't know either, but was looking into it as much as she could. She was more interested in whether or not Detective Hampton was any closer in getting visas to Canada. Aine explained that it was not decided as yet, and that she wouldn't know until after the trial. The detective was under pressure from his boss, and Aunt Hettie understood.

"Aine?" Detective Hampton said, bringing her back from her thoughts.

"Okay, I am ready," Aine said, picking up her handbag. "Let's nail him and get this over with." Aine noticed that she hadn't put Anchorette's jewellery in with the rest of her belongings, which were all packed up in boxes and ready for the move. She would just have to take the jewellery to court with her.

Detective Hampton signalled for her and a guard to follow him, and they headed to the car that was parked furthest outside in the drive. The other car would be for Keith and the social worker. The driver for her car was already seated, and a woman was seated in the front passenger seat. In the back was another man. Aine looked at Detective Hampton.

"I will follow in a separate car, Aine, and will be right behind you. You will be safe in the car," he said, reassuring her as she sat down in the middle seat and buckled herself up. The guard got in next to her and she was sandwiched between the two men.

"Ready?" the driver asked.

"Yes," the guard who followed in after Aine answered.

The engine turned and thrummed to life as the driver put the car into first and drove down the drive. Aine's heartbeat picked up pace as the car accelerated towards the city. It was on days like today that she wished she could have a hit of drugs. Anything to take the edge off or help her forget altogether. But because of Dean and what he had done to her Brett, she knew she had to face him. It made her so angry that her heartbeat sped up even faster and she used her anger to keep it there.

Aine's anger made the journey seem faster. The city, as usual, was busy with everyday life. People were travelling in every direction possible. Aine knew that the path she was on today was coming to a close. Sitting in court and waiting her turn was difficult.

"Aine," a voice whispered. Aine looked up to see her Aunt Hettie standing across the hall. "Head to the bathroom to your right. I need to talk to you right now," Aunt Hettie said, walking to the bathroom.

Aine sighed. "Excuse me, guard, but my bladder has chosen that now would be the time to make its own personal appearance." She nodded in Aunt Hettie's direction. The guard followed her gaze and nodded once, not seeing anyone else. "Thanks, won't be a minute," Aine said, and followed Aunt Hettie into the bathroom. She opened the door and went into a stall. "This better be good," Aine whispered.

"We know how the shadow slayers have been finding Anchorette and keeping tabs on you as well," Aunt Hettie said, not wasting time. "Joe's father gave Anchorette her wedding ring, claiming that it had belonged to Joe's mother. It has a tracking device built into the gold. The jewellery you picked up at the house could also contain tracking devices," Aunt Hettie finished.

"Oh, shit," Aine said she opened her handbag. There the jewellery stared right back at them. Aine turned to the toilet cistern and lifted the lid. She put the lid on top of the toilet seat and tipped the jewellery into the cistern "Well, that's my end dealt with, but how do I get to Anchorette before she leaves the hospital?" Aine asked Aunt Hettie.

"Not sure, but you shall have to move fast. I have to go— they are calling me on the other side," Aunt Hettie said. She started to fade, knowing she was leaving Aine in the lurch once again.

"Aine Hews to courtroom two, please," Aine heard over the intercom speaker.

"Well, that is creepy," Aine muttered as she lifted the lid off the seat and placed it back into position. She left the bathroom and saw Detective Hampton on the phone.

"Is she ready to go?" he asked into the phone.

Aine couldn't help but wonder if the fates were having a hand at helping her today. "Is that Anchorette?" Aine asked. Detective Hampton nodded. "I need to speak to her now." Aine wasn't asking: she was demanding.

Detective Hampton looked at her. "Hang on a second, Miss Hews would like to speak to her sister." Detective Hampton wasn't going to argue. He knew Aine was not messing about, and instinct told him she wouldn't give up. "Here you go, but make it quick," Detective Hampton said, passing the phone.

Aine took it from him and turned her back to him. She knew it was rude, but she didn't care for manners at that precise second.

"Anchorette, listen carefully. You know the item Mr. Miller gave you claiming it was from his late wife? You have to remove it. Leave it in the hospital. Do you understand me?" Aine spoke as quietly as she could.

"I understand," Anchorette said. "Good luck today, and see you soon."

"See you soon," Aine said before handing the phone back to Detective Hampton. "I am ready now," Aine said, feeling the anger flaring inside her once again.

Chapter Thirty-Two

Aine

The interior of the courtroom was very grand, with the woodwork made of mahogany and the seats made of the same wood and red leather.

Dean was in the dock looking right at her. He knew he was in trouble and that she was going to send him down for a long time.

The prosecutor for the crown started off first by asking Aine the questions that she already knew were coming. Detective Hampton had taken extra time to prepare her, but they didn't know what the defence team would be asking.

"Miss Hews, for how long have you known the defendant?" the prosecutor asked. He was in his mid-forties and had a round face and belly. His face was serious, as though he had little time or patience for anything.

"I have known Dean—I mean, Mr. Hunter—since we were in high school. I had seen him around. But I didn't actually talk to him until I started dating his brother Brett," Aine answered.

The questions came in thick and fast, and Aine answered them all with ease. The defence team jotted down notes and listened. It was uncomfortable being watched, but Aine knew that this would be the easy bit.

The prosecutor laid his questions to rest. Dean's defence lawyer stepped up, a thin man with a long, thin face. He too had an appearance of intolerance of the world of fun and was clearly going to grill her under more pressure.

"Tell me, Miss Hews, what was my client's reputation as a pupil in high school?" he asked.

"He was popular. All the girls would surround him," Aine answered.

"And Mr. Hunter's brother, Brett. What was his reputation at school?" the lawyer asked.

"He was quiet, the complete opposite of Dean. Very shy and awkward at times."

"Now would you please tell the court what you were like in high school, please?" Aine knew this was coming.

"I was a difficult teenager. I drank and hardly turned up at school towards the end. Anyone who knew me in the town I grew up in knew that. Yes, I also did drugs at the time to annoy my parents and escape their controlling ways," Aine answered as truthfully as she could.

"Is it fair to say you were a troublesome teenager who stole and lied to fund your drug habit?" the defence lawyer asked.

"I wouldn't say it was fair. I would say it was the accurate truth," Aine answered.

The defence lawyer smirked at her. He disliked her a lot.

"Please tell the court, Miss Hews, how you and the deceased Brett started dating."

"We met at a nightclub. He was sitting in the corner drinking by himself. His brother Dean was also there, but Dean was with a group of people, one of whom I now know to be my sister's father-in-law. I talked to Brett that evening, and we got to know one another. It was a good evening. He had some drugs and we went back to his place. We were inseparable from that point on," Aine said.

The defence nodded. Aine could tell where this was going. Detective Hampton had told her that the defence team would try to make her look as bad as they possibly could. Which, to be fair, wasn't a difficult job when she looked at it.

"Were you two inseparable because he had an endless supply of drugs, or because it was love?" the lawyer asked. His tone was mocking now, as if Aine had been a silly little lost child.

"It was drugs at first, I admit to that. However, there was a side to Brett that was frightened. He didn't tell me of whom he was frightened, but now I know," Aine said, answering as truthfully as she could and trying to make Dean look as bad as possible. She couldn't resist looking at Dean; his knuckles were white and tightly clenched. He was angry as hell, she could see it. His jaw muscles clenched as he chewed the inside of his cheek. Aine stared straight at him and raised her right eyebrow. Suddenly Dean stood up with his veins popping from his neck, screaming, "You fucking slut, you never loved my brother. You were only ever after the endless drugs he supplied. You wouldn't leave him alone and he wouldn't leave me alone, constantly tapping me for a hit. You should have died right along with Dean that night, but we didn't get the chance," Dean blurted out.

"ORDER IN THE COURT PLEASE," the judge shouted, hitting his gavel.

Aine sat in the witness seat, jaw half open at the confession Dean had just made. The gavel drummed away to her right as the judge shouted and the two barristers approached the bench to speak. Had she heard correctly? Had Dean intended to kill her as well that night? Her head was buzzing and her lips became numb. One of the security guards suddenly leapt in front of her. Blood spattered across Aine's neck and blouse. The guard had been hit by a bullet. Where it came from Aine had no idea. All Aine knew was to get her ass out of the seat she was in and hide behind the witness box. She pushed herself out of her chair and got to her knees, pulling the chair close to her for something to hold on to. Her breathing was shaky and she was panicking. Dean's words were still buzzing around in her head. What had he meant when he said about something stopping him? She knew now was a time to focus. To her left Detective Hampton came into her line of sight: he had made his way around the judge's seat. He had a bullet vest in one hand and a handgun in the other.

"Here, put this on," he said, passing the vest to her. Aine took it, her hands shaking, and slipped it on, making sure the Velcro was tight.

"At my nod we are going to move to the back to where the judge came out. Do not stop—just focus on the door, Aine. Do you understand?" Detective Hampton asked. Aine nodded. As soon as Detective Hampton moved the chair and Aine crawled out, she could see the judge and a guard standing right in front of her, their eyes blank.

"Oh, crap," Aine said when she realized that the judge and guard were looking at their own dead bodies lying on the floor.

"Move, Aine, now," Detective Hampton said, pushing her past them. Aine started moving, keeping her eyes focused on finding the door. Detective Hampton guided her towards it.

"Wait, Aine," the detective said. He pushed the judge's chair a little and a bang went off. There was still a shooter in the room.

"I can't see him," Detective Hampton said. "He must be hidden somewhere up in the gallery." Aine looked around. She focused on the guard standing over the judge.

"If something right now would like to give us a little help here as to where the shooter is, that would be real helpful," Aine said quietly. The guard and judge both turned around. Aine smiled at them. "Yes, some help would be good," Aine said again.

Detective Hampton looked at her. "I am working on it as we speak, Aine, but it's going to take time," Detective Hampton said.

"I'm sure help is on its way." Aine smiled again, looking at the guard. The guard, without thinking, walked towards the stairs to the gallery and climbed up. He looked down the rows, searching for the shooter. He looked back towards her and pointed at a seat in the second row.

"Get down," Detective Hampton said, pulling her back down.

"Detective, would you believe me if I said I knew where the shooter was hiding?" Aine asked.

"Right now I am beginning to think you need that vacation of a lifetime in Canada," the detective replied.

Aine raised her eyebrow. "Aim for the second row to the right—the sixth, maybe seventh seat in from the middle left," Aine said. She looked at the detective, challenging him. He swallowed.

"How do you know this?" he asked.

"Intuition," Aine answered. It was a stupid answer, but what else could she say?

Detective Hampton looked at her, wondering if she was right or not. He checked his gun; he still had three bullets left. He took in a few short breaths. He didn't know, but his inner self told him she was right. He breathed in again slowly and calmly, closing his eyes. He then moved quickly for someone of his size and age and fired one shot. The gunshot echoed, and it took a while for silence to fill the court again. Aine waited for the guard to give her a signal of some sort, but instead it was the judge who spoke.

"Robert says the detective hit his shooting arm, but he is waiting for your next move."

Aine nodded. Her lips formed a thin smile of appreciation at knowing it must have been such a difficult time for him.

"I think we should make something move to see if he is down," Aine said to the detective.

"Intuition telling you that, or your common sense?" the detective asked, laughing. He grabbed the judge's chair and moved it just enough, but nothing happened.

"I think he is down," the detective said, moving to the judge's door. A round of bullets fired out, echoing across the room. Aine reached out and pulled the detective back to where they had been hiding. He slumped against her.

"Oh shit, oh shit," Aine said, panicking. He had been hit in the right shoulder, and the bullet had gone through his back. He was not breathing right. Aine grabbed the gun he had dropped to the floor and looked at the judge.

"He is still in the same place Robert is pointing to," he said.

"I have never fired a gun before," Aine said. She put the detective into a lying position to her side. She saw the detective's radio attached to his bullet vest. She grabbed hold of it and started pressing the button and talking into it.

"Hello, Detective Hampton is down and I'm in the courtroom with a shooter. Hello, is anyone there?" Aine asked. No one answered. She waited, but no one replied. It didn't make sense—what could be happening outside that would prevent someone from responding? Aine sat, thinking. If she waited a little while longer, maybe someone would come for her. But the shooter could by then make his move, and she couldn't take that chance. The detective couldn't wait that much longer, either. She had to make a choice.

"Fuck it," she said loud enough for the shooter to hear. She knew he would be tempted, and she also knew that she had two bullets left, so if the first one didn't hit she would make sure the second one did before his first one hit her. She heard him chuckling and taunting her.

"Got to give it to you, Aine. You're nothing like your sister. She hasn't got the guts and courage you have shown so far," the shooter said.

"Trouble with you is that you don't know what you're talking about, shadow slayer," Aine said.

"So you know what I am. Very good—how did you find out?" the shadow slayer asked.

"It doesn't matter. You wanted me, so finish it off," Aine said. She looked at the judge, waiting for his signal from Robert the guard.

"Now," the judge said to Aine.

She turned in the direction of the shooter and fired the gun once.

"She shot him in the leg," the guard said.

"How's that leg doing there, shadow slayer?" She could hear grunting and material ripping.

"You will pay for that, bitch. Or should I say, slut. Joe told me what he carved into your back." The shadow slayer sneered at Aine. Aine's stomach churned. This shadow slayer personally knew her through Joe.

"Call me whatever you like, shadow slayer, but you won't be walking out of here alive," Aine said, not letting her fear show in her voice.

"He is moving to your left, Aine. I can see him, and he will see you soon if you don't move around my desk now," the judge said. Aine stepped over the detective and crawled to the side of the judge's desk. Robert's body was lying close to where she was, and Aine saw his gun in his right hand. She wondered if she could reach it without the shadow slayer shooting her. Aine stretched out to grab it.

"He is thinking about climbing down," Robert shouted.

Aine took the gun in her hand and waited.

"Get ready," the judge said.

"No, wait, he is changing his move. It's a bomb—he is going to throw a grenade," Robert shouted.

Aine peeked up over the judge's desk. She saw the shooter's hand about to throw the grenade. She fired the guard's gun, not knowing how many bullets were left in it. The shadow slayer screamed out in pain, and the grenade clattered onto the ground next to him.

"Cover your ears," the judge screamed. Aine covered her ears and the grenade exploded. The courtroom shook, and plaster and debris fell all around Aine. She moved back to where the detective was and pulled him and herself under the judge's desk, protecting him as best she could.

Aine kept the gun in her hand, not sure if the shooter was still alive. The door to the judge's chambers opened and Aine aimed the gun, not sure who would be stepping through.

"Miss Hews, Detective Hampton, can you hear us? It's security." Aine waited, not responding. She could hear rubble being moved and feet walking past the judge's table. Her hand shook when a pair of legs stopped in front of the judge's desk. An armed security guard bent down.

"Over here," he shouted. "It's okay, Miss Hews, you will be all right now. Please put the gun down."

She looked up to see the judge and Robert, the other guard.

"You can trust them, they work here," the judge said.

"Thank you," Aine said, and with that the judge and Robert faded away.

Chapter Thirty-Three

Anchorette

Leaving the hospital to safety seemed like a dream to Anchorette. It had been so tedious being trapped in hospital after hospital with security guards watching her every move, which hadn't been much in a hospital bed. The nurses helping her into the car were kind in wishing her well and a speedy recovery. How she would exit the car at the safe house she wasn't sure. One of the security guards passed her a phone. She looked at him, confused, as his expression was one of annoyance.

"Hello?" Anchorette asked.

"Anchorette, listen carefully. You know the item Mr. Miller gave you claiming it was from his late wife? You have to remove it. Leave it in the hospital. Do you understand me?" Aine said.

"I understand," Anchorette said, looking at the wedding ring on her finger. "Good luck today, and see you soon."

"See you soon," Aine said. "I am ready now," Anchorette heard Aine say as the line was disconnected. She handed the phone back to the guard. He took it, looking at her. She smiled at him as she rubbed her right finger and thumb over her wedding band.

"Would you mind doing me a small favour, please?" she asked the security guard. He looked at her, waiting for her to carry on. He was clearly not one with a sense of humour.

"Could I have this window down? I'm feeling a little carsick. It has been a while since I last travelled in one and, well, that did not end so well," Anchorette said. She had intended to ask him to just place the ring in the bin, but she didn't know if he would or wouldn't, and so thought she would wait till the car was moving.

"Of course, Mrs. Miller," the guard said, closing the car door. Anchorette hated hearing her married name; it made her feel sick and angry. The guard walked around to the other side of the car. Anchorette had by then wound down the window, and she placed her left hand on the window as the guard got in. The guard sat down and spoke to the driver in front of him to let him know that they were ready to leave.

The car started rolling forward, and as it did Anchorette's finger and thumb trembled. She knew she was letting go of many things that had been built upon lies and betrayal. But she wouldn't let go of her kids, and knew she had to put them first. She dropped the ring out the window, and then placed both her hands over her belly, rubbing and soothing her unborn child. She was excited that soon she would be reunited with her son and sister. It had been so hard not to resent her sister for being there for her son when she should have been there instead. But Joe had tried to stop her from being all that she was to Keith: a loving mother.

The car was picking up pace now as it headed east. The motorway was not as busy as it could have been—weekday traffic could be unpredictable, and traffic jams could have happened—so they travelled along at a steady pace. The guard's phone started buzzing and he answered it. He was short in his answers, and when he stated that Anchorette was still safe he didn't make her feel well. The guard hung up and spoke to the driver, insisting that he speed up and move to the safe house as quickly as possible.

"What's wrong?" Anchorette asked the guard. She didn't look away from him as she waited for his reply.

"There has been trouble at the courthouse, and we need to get both you and your son safely to the house," the guard answered. Anchorette's thoughts raced in all directions. Her son, was he safe? What had happened to Aine—was she alive? What would happen if she was not, or if Joe had somehow kidnapped Keith? No wait, Joe was still in prison, wasn't he?

"Is Joe still in prison?" Anchorette asked.

"Yes, as far as I know," the guard answered.

"What happened at the courthouse?" Anchorette asked, feeling sick. Her lips felt numb and her breathing became short and rapid.

"Mrs. Miller, please try to remain calm, or we shall have to turn around and return you to the hospital in your condition," the guard answered.

"I'm Miss Hews—don't ever call me Mrs. Miller again. Now tell me what has happened to my sister," Anchorette said, all but shouting right in the guard's face.

The guard looked at Anchorette directly in the face. "Miss Hews, please calm yourself down. I do not know what is happening at the courthouse. Detective Hampton will call back when it has been resolved," he said as firmly as he could. Anchorette breathed slowly and deeply. She knew it was not his fault, but he should have gotten more information from Detective Hampton before he hung up.

"I'm sorry," Anchorette said after a few moments of silence.

The guard looked at her and nodded, and then looked back to the motorway. Anchorette was frustrated, for the journey just didn't seem to end and the phone didn't buzz again. The driver took a series of left and right turns. Anchorette wasn't focused on where she was headed; they weren't in the city anymore, just along a motorway. She hoped Aine was safe and Keith was already at the safe house.

It would be another ten minutes before she knew if Keith had arrived safely. The driver pulled up a drive to what looked like a five- or six-bedroom house. She wasn't taking it all in properly. The guard got out of his side and walked around to Anchorette's side of the car, where she was already attempting to get out. The months she had sat in the hospital bed had made her bones a little too relaxed, and the nurses had told her that mobility would be slow to come back. But she was determined to get up on her feet as quickly as possible. The guard noted her determination but also had to make sure she was safe.

"Miss Hews, if you wouldn't mind accepting my offer of help?" he said, extending his hand to help her up. Anchorette looked up and grasped his outstretched hand.

"Thank you," she said, taking his hand and pulling herself out of the car. She turned to the front door of the house. It was just a plain white front door, but it led to what would be her home for a while at least. She let go of the guard's hand, feeling she had her balance. She let him lead her while the front passenger guard walked right behind her. The door opened automatically, and all three walked into a hallway entrance and then into the sitting room. It was large, with a huge sofa and two chairs. Anchorette felt she would be safest in one of the chairs. The sofa would most certainly swamp her.

"Your son will be arriving shortly, Miss Hews," the guard said as she positioned herself into the chair.

"Is he safe? And do you have any word on Aine yet?" Anchorette blurted out the questions hurriedly, fearing the guard would walk off before she could ask.

"Your son is safe, but no word on what is happening at the courthouse yet," the guard said. "Would you like something to drink?" he suggested. Anchorette thought about it; some fluid was perhaps a good idea.

"Some water, please. My throat is a little dry," Anchorette answered.

The guard walked off to her left and came back with a clear glass of water. She accepted it with a smile and took a sip. The sip turned into long gulps. She had no idea she was so thirsty. The guard looked at her, surprised. Anchorette finished.

"Thank you," Anchorette said, not sure what else to say or do. She felt awkward being in a house with armed men and waiting for her son and news of her sister. The house wasn't exactly homely. It was just four walls with the essentials, and it lacked warmth. The guard's phone buzzed again. He answered it and spoke one word: "Okay." He put the phone away and looked at Anchorette. "Your son is here," he said. Anchorette looked around to find somewhere to put her empty glass and noticed a coffee table between the two chairs. She placed the glass on the table and started to move out of her chair.

"No, you stay here. We will bring your son to you," the guard said. Anchorette supposed it made sense. She heard the front door opening and feet shuffling in. A guard came in first, followed by a woman holding Keith in her arms. Anchorette's heart leapt with happiness. The social worker walked over to Anchorette, whose arms were outstretched and ready to take Keith into a warm hug. She placed Keith into Anchorette's arms. Keith giggled with happiness. But the happiness was short-lived. The guard's phone buzzed again, and Anchorette knew it must be news of the courthouse. The guard was on the phone longer this time, giving a series of yeses and nos with some okays added in. The social worker waited with Anchorette to see what the guard had to say. He hung up.

"Aine is fine, a little shaken up, but fine and alive," he began. "Detective Hampton has been seriously injured and is being taken to the hospital for an emergency operation. Detective Bells will be arriving with Aine at some point today. I can't say anything else yet. You, Miss Hews, and your son will be on lockdown and not allowed to go anywhere without an armed guard." He turned to go and deliver the news to the other armed guards surrounding the house.

"Hello, Mrs. Miller, I am Keith's social worker, Miss Deltab. Your son has been through just as much of a trauma as you and your sister. But I'm sure with the right kind of guidance he shall turn out to be just a normal boy who won't remember any of this," Miss Deltab said while smiling kindly at Anchorette. Anchorette was ready to explode, but she kept her anger firmly in control and didn't say anything. She sat playing with Keith on her lap. The stitches had not been long removed; the doctor had been surprised at how quickly she had healed up. But her skin was still tender.

It was late afternoon before any sort of activity happened. Anchorette had told the social worker that she was going to take an afternoon nap with Keith. She had carried Keith up the stairs, which had hurt her a bit, and lay in bed with Keith in the cot bed next to her. One of the armed guards upstairs had pointed her in the direction of her and Keith's room. Their belongings were already there. Somehow Aine's items had also ended up in the same room, not that it mattered much.

Anchorette and Keith rested well for a few hours. Anchorette was glad to have escaped from the social worker, who had constantly been telling her what her son liked to do and did not like to do. How Aine had tolerated her Anchorette would never know. She woke up to the sound of a knock on her bedroom door.

"Come in," Anchorette answered groggily. It was the guard who had travelled with her that morning.

"Miss Hews, your sister will be arriving shortly. She has some cuts and bruises and is a little traumatized, but she is safe and well," the guard said. Anchorette got up from her bed and looked over to see Keith in his cot bed, smiling and happy to see her. She picked him up and they went back down the stairs. Anchorette looked around for the social worker.

"Are you looking for Miss Deltab?" the guard asked. Anchorette nodded. "She left, as she was called to another emergency," he said. Anchorette let out a long breath. Both the guard and Anchorette went back to the sitting room. Anchorette sat in the same chair with Keith in her arms, waiting again. Anchorette felt uncomfortable and smiled a few times at the guard, but he was not the easiest to get along with. His personality was cold, and she didn't see a wedding band on his finger.

Finally the front door opened and Anchorette heard footsteps. A woman came in first.

"Detective Bells," the guard said. Aine followed with an armed guard behind her. Aine ran to Anchorette and embraced Anchorette and Keith.

"You're safe," Anchorette said with relief. Aine stepped back. Anchorette could see the cuts and scrapes on her head and arms. The blood didn't appear to be all from her. Anchorette kept looking her over and over to see where all the blood had come from.

"It's not mine, Anchorette. It is Detective Hampton's and another guard's," Aine said, seeing that Anchorette was looking her over. "I'm safe and fine, really. It's Detective Hampton we have to wait and see about."

The house was a hive of constant activity over the next week, with guards coming and going. Some faces became familiar to Anchorette and Aine. Detective Bells came by the day after the attack at the courthouse to get a statement from Aine as to what had happened to them in court. Of course she had already explained everything to Anchorette as best she could without making herself sound crazy as hell. Her hands had been shaking the whole time. Anchorette was horrified that Joe had somehow been caught up in it all.

The news came through that Detective Hampton had come through the operation but was looking at possible early retirement. Aine had been smart in saving his life, the doctors had said. She hadn't known it, but she had been holding on to him so tightly under the judge's chair that she had stemmed the flow of blood. She hadn't even known.

At the beginning of the week, Detective Bells came to the safe house. Anchorette and Aine sat in the chairs, with Keith in Aine's arms. Detective Bells sat on the edge of the sofa. She opened her briefcase and set out some paperwork.

"Detective Hampton asked me to pass on his gratitude to you, Miss Aine. He also said that you have asked to be given new identities and lives and that you are both thinking of Canada," Detective Bells said, looking at the sisters. Aine and Anchorette smiled at each other. "It would appear your request has been granted, but on the condition that Aine gives evidence against Joe Miller." Detective Bells waited for Aine's response.

"Yes, I will give evidence just as soon as you get Anchorette and Keith safely out of here," Aine said.

Detective Bells smiled. "I'm not up for bargaining here, Miss Hews. That might have worked with Detective Hampton, but I don't do it. You will give evidence against Joe Miller when summoned, and Mrs. Miller and her son will be sent with or without you when we decide to send them, not when you tell us to," Detective Bells said firmly.

"Your new identities will be as follows: Aine, your name is now Sharon Shephard, born the twelfth of February, 1976. Anchorette, your name is now Shelby Shephard, born the fifteenth of June, 1978. Your son, Keith—"

"Just hang on a second," said Aine. "We are not changing our names or our birthdates, and we are not bargaining on that either. If Joe intends to find us he will do so. Just give us a head start in leaving the country. All I asked from Detective Hampton was to move us out to Canada. We can look after ourselves after that, please."

Anchorette knew Aine was right. If Joe had any intention of finding them, then he would. Not that Detective Bells would grasp that.

"Look, I get that it is a little too much right now to take in, but you girls will need new identities. You can't leave here with your names—they are not common enough and are too easily recognizable," Detective Bells said, trying to calm the situation.

"Perhaps we could just use the names for identity purposes and for public appearances, Aine," Anchorette said, encouraging Aine to go along with it.

"Okay, but those names are awful," Aine said.

"I shall leave the information here for you two to look over and memorize. It has details of your parents' backgrounds and where you were born," Detective Bells said.

"How is Detective Hampton doing in the hospital?" Anchorette asked.

"He is recuperating well. We won't know much else until the end of the week. Detective Hampton doesn't, it would appear, remember much of what happened, just that he felt himself falling backward and you catching him and keeping him safe," Detective Bells said.

"Well, it's good to know that he is coming through this well," Aine said, feeling uncomfortable and not wanting to relive the whole nightmare again.

"Do you know when the trial for Joe will be taking place?" Aine asked, trying to avoid any more talk of the court appearance.

"Well, with Dean Hunter having been killed, we will be pushing your evidence, Aine, that you recognized Joe's father in the nightclub and that the drugs Joe used on you matched the drugs in the warehouse that belonged to Dean Hunter. But I don't know just yet when this case will be heard. You will have to wait it out here till the courthouse, or at least part of it, is ready. That grenade the shooter used caused a lot of damage. The papers have, of course, been reporting about the events and the explosion. Miss Hews, we are doing our best to keep your name, as well as Mrs. Miller's name, out of the papers, but it is not easy. Someone has already phoned the newspaper a few times dropping your names," Detective Bells said.

"Well, it wasn't us," Aine said

"We know it was not either of you. Joe is, of course, being watched and monitored closely. We had a development yesterday that we are unsure about," Detective Bells said, watching Aine and Anchorette's responses.

"Well, don't stop there, Detective. Either spit it out or not," Aine said, becoming impatient. Anchorette shifted her weight from one side to the other, trying to get comfortable.

"Well, the prison service phoned through yesterday to tell me that Lindsey was found dead in her cell. We are at this time not sure what caused her death, but the postmortem is due back soon, so hopefully we shall know more on that. Also, a female body was found in the river in the city this morning. We believe this to be the woman who was the accomplice to Lindsey at the hospital and who tried to kidnap your son," Detective Bells said.

Aine looked at Anchorette. "You believe it to be her? How are you sure it is her?" Aine asked.

"I'm glad she is dead," Anchorette said before the detective could answer. The detective looked stunned. Anchorette didn't have a bad bone in her body and had never before wished harm on anyone.

"Anchorette, I'm sure you don't mean that," Aine said, looking at her.

"Don't I? She wrecked my marriage. She pretended to be my friend and tried to have me killed, and on top of that she tried to steal my son. You bet I do mean it. If it is her friend that you dragged out of the river, I hope she suffered just as much as I have these past two months. My son has been through enough," Anchorette said as she got up and walked over to Aine. "Keith needs his dinner. I will take him into the kitchen. I have heard enough," Anchorette finished, taking Keith out of Aine's arms.

Aine didn't stop her. She understood the hurt that Anchorette was feeling and understood the hatred as well, even if it did frighten her that Anchorette was showing it so visibly. Both Aine and the detective waited till Anchorette had left before they carried on.

"So, how do you know it was the same woman?" Aine asked.

"We had the social worker come in this morning to identify the body. She believes it could possibly be her. But we would also like you to come down tomorrow and identify her. It's just so we know there was not a third woman out there that we missed," Detective Bells said.

"Do I have to? I just had my fair share of dead bodies last week," Aine answered.

"I'm sorry, but yes, you do," the detective said, getting up and gathering her things together.

"We will send a car for you, and a guard will escort you to and from the morgue. Please be ready early tomorrow," the detective said. "I had expected your sister's reaction. I know that if I were in her position, I would be feeling the same and would have reacted the same way." The detective left Aine sitting alone in her chair.

As soon as the detective was gone, Aine followed Anchorette into the kitchen. Keith was sitting in a high chair and singing his own little song, unaware that his mother was crying while cooking his dinner. Aine walked up behind Anchorette and put her arms around her. She didn't need to say anything: a hug was all that was needed. The house was quiet that evening, with Aine dreading the following day at the morgue.

Chapter Thirty-Four

Aine

The next day Aine had gotten up early as requested and was sitting in the car with the guard who had escorted Anchorette from the hospital. Anchorette had commented on the first night they were back together on how frosty his personality was. She had not been wrong. Aine had had warmer welcomes from Jack Frost on wintry mornings. But it suited her fine, as she knew the morgue would be the complete opposite: loud, and filled with spirits.

Aine plugged in her iPod and pressed play. As they travelled along the highway she listened to Rob Zombie; she had managed to download *Hellbilly*. She sat with her eyes closed, trying to remain calm.

The guard poked her on the arm to gain her attention. Aine opened her eyes and pulled out her earbuds.

"We are here, Miss Hews," the guard said.

"Okay." Aine rolled her eyes as she looked through the window and saw all sorts of spirits from different eras of time. She stepped out of the car as the door was opened for her. To her surprise, Detective Bells was there to see here through this.

"Good morning, Miss Hews," the detective said.

"Morning," Aine said. The guard and Aine followed the detective through the entrance and into the waiting area. The receptionist sat there with her most sympathetic expression.

"I am Detective Bells. We are here to identify the body of the woman pulled out of the river on Sunday."

The receptionist picked up the phone to place a call. Aine took a seat and waited while the guard stood to her side. The number of spirits there was beyond anything Aine had ever seen. They were all just wandering around. They seemed to be lost and yet not looking for anyone in particular.

A man opened a security-coded door and smiled.

"You here to identify the woman from this Sunday?" he asked.

"Yes, I am Detective Bells," she said, showing her badge. "And this is Miss Hews."

"This way then, please," the man said. "Unfortunately she has suffered quite a fair beating and took in quite a lot of water."

The guard and Aine followed the man into a room. The detective stood close to the door and didn't come into the room. The room felt very surgical and clinical. In the centre of it was a table covered with a white sheet.

"Are you ready?" the man asked Aine.

Aine nodded, clenching her teeth

The sheet was pulled back. Aine's stomach rolled.

"Is it her?" the detective asked.

"Yes, it's her," Aine said, feeling the room spinning. The guard gripped her arm to steady her. He guided her out of the room and back into the corridor.

"Anchorette got her wish. She suffered," Aine said.

"Yes, she did, but now we need to figure out how and who," Detective Bells said.

"Can I take a step outside, please?" Aine asked.

"Thank you," the detective said to the man before they all headed back outside to the cars.

As if Aine's morning could possibly get any worse, she saw standing by her car door both Lindsey and her cousin Lacey.

"You won't win," Lindsey said.

"Joe will get his kids back," Lacey taunted Aine.

Aine knew she couldn't react, what with the guard and Detective Bells standing right next to her.

The vision in front of Aine warped, and out stepped Aunt Hettie along with six other spirits.

"Lindsey and Lacey O'Donnell, you are hereby charged with the attempted murder of Mrs. Anchorette Miller and the kidnapping of Keith Miller," Aunt Hettie said clearly.

The six spirits surrounded Lindsey and Lacey with long spears. At the end of each spear glowed a different-coloured stone. Lindsey tried to push past the spirits but couldn't.

"What's happening, Lindsey?" asked Lacey. *Good question*, thought Aine, as she couldn't very well ask aloud.

Each spirit chanted and murmured as the tips of the spears glowed brighter. They became so bright it was hard to see the spirits of Lindsey and Lacey. Then in a flash of bright light, all of the spirits, including Aunt Hettie, disappeared. Aine squinted, shaking her head.

"Are you all right?" Detective Bells asked.

"Yes, sorry, just feeling a little sick still, and my eyes are not focusing properly," Aine answered.

"Yes, I felt exactly the same way the first time I saw a dead body," Detective Bells said.

Aine looked at her, confused for a second. Then she remembered Lacey's body and leaned over, throwing up.

"I did that as well," Detective Bells said sympathetically.

The drive back to the safe house was quiet, with the guard not saying a single word. When they pulled up to the house Aine waited till the guard opened her car door.

"You did well today, Miss Hews," he said. Aine, shocked, looked at him and raised an eyebrow. He nodded towards the front door. They walked into the house with another guard behind Aine.

"Was it her?" Anchorette asked as Aine entered the sitting room.

"It was," Aine said. "If you will excuse me for a second or two, I need to take a long shower." Aine left the room.

"Take it easy on her, Miss Hews, she has been through a lot today," the guard said before leaving the room. Anchorette was stunned. She didn't understand and was mad as hell. She followed the guard.

"What do you mean?" Anchorette asked, catching up to him.

"I mean, she saw a body today after seeing bodies fall before her last week. She is still recovering from the use of drugs, and all you want to know is if it was the woman or not. I would say she has had a lot of pressure to handle. Not to say that you don't yourself, Miss Hews. However, it is just an observation," the guard said. He nodded once and left Anchorette standing in the kitchen.

She was not sure if she was more stunned that the guard had just told her off or that he had spoken to her at all.

Anchorette flipped the switch on the kettle and grabbed two mugs out of the cupboard. Keith had only been down for a short while for his afternoon nap. She waited for the kettle to boil and made one cup of coffee and a cup of tea. Anchorette passed one of the guards in the hallway before going upstairs. She smiled at him. They never seemed to speak to either her or her sister and never had anything to do with Keith; they were always on the job. It was comforting but also unsettling at the same time. Anchorette placed the mug of coffee in Aine's bedroom and sat on Aine's bed with her tea. She waited till Aine was finished with her shower. Anchorette could hear Aine crying and knew she had a lot to be thankful for and sorry for.

Aine came out a short while later. Anchorette smiled a little, and Aine sat on the bed next to her and laid her head down on her lap.

"I'm sorry I didn't think of how stressful this has been for you," Anchorette said. "I have been so angry over the last couple days. I don't want to lose you or Keith, and I know Joe will be planning something. The fact that Lindsey and Lacey are both dead does not bode well for us either. I'm frightened."

Tears began to run down Aine's face. "I'm frightened for you, Anchorette. I had never seen you angry before, and what was done to Lacey I wouldn't wish on anyone regardless of what they tried to do," Aine said.

"Was it that bad?" Anchorette asked.

"Yes. Whatever it was they used on her, it was bad. I would hope to go quickly. She suffered. All I am trying to do is save us all. My timing may be unintended, but it's all I can do and all that I am able to do right now." The sisters didn't say anything else; they just sat on the bed thinking to themselves and spending time together.

That evening the girls were preparing dinner in the kitchen with Keith when the unfriendly guard walked in.

"That was Detective Bells. A court date has been set for next week. Miss Aine, you will be due to appear on

Wednesday. Miss Anchorette, you will be leaving this Friday for the airport with Keith to catch a flight to Canada."

The girls looked at each other. "This Friday? But today is Tuesday," Anchorette said.

"Yes, it is. But Detective Bells will also need to prepare Miss Aine for the trial next week," the guard said.

"That's it, then. I guess we should start packing this evening." The girls turned and carried on cooking. The last days together would mean a lot, and they both knew it.

Wednesday came and went with laughter and distractions, and Thursday came all too soon for Anchorette's liking. The packing and the tearful moments made the evening stressful. Aine didn't know what to take from the house, and as it was, Anchorette was growing bigger. Aine slept in the same room as Anchorette and Keith, but neither Aine nor Anchorette slept well.

Of course they were not alone. Grandmama Hartwood and Aunt Hettie had come in for a get-together with Aine and Anchorette.

Anchorette fell in and out of sleep, the baby taking a toll on her body.

"So I take it you can't explain to me what Tuesday was all about, then?" Aine asked Aunt Hettie.

"No, you can't. All you need to know is that Lindsey and Lacey can no longer harm you, your children, or the generations after them," Grandmama Hartwood said, looking at Keith. "He is taking a stretch again in height," she noted

"He is not the only one taking a stretch. Have you seen how big Anchorette is getting?" Aine commented.

"A pregnant woman is a beautiful sight, and don't you ever forget that," Grandmama Hartwood said, smiling at her granddaughter's belly.

Eventually Aine fell asleep. Grandmama Hartwood and Aunt Hettie left after wishing them both safe journeys until they met again.

It was difficult for Aine to see Anchorette leave with Keith the next morning. It had not helped that Detective Bells had to pull out all the stops, for the newspapers had put the courtroom explosion on their front pages, along with their names and pictures. Their mother Janet had spoken to the press, so Detective Bells had to set up a decoy for Anchorette at the airport to take off some of the stress.

"Are you sure it will be safe for her at the airport?" Aine asked Detective Bells.

"Yes, we already have the plans in motion. All Anchorette has to do is listen and follow the plan," Detective Bells said. "Now we should start preparing for the trial on Wednesday," she said, sitting down on the sofa.

Chapter Thirty-Five

Joe

Joe sat in the prison van waiting for the other prisoner to get in. The chains on his wrists and ankles were on tightly, so escape was not going to happen.

The door slammed shut and the engine started. Joe was going to court for his trial, and he didn't know what he was going to do or say. Martin had not shown up, and there was no news from his father. He had seen the papers and had seen what Janet had said. He had hoped that she would blame it on Aine.

The van sped up down the street and the brakes screeched suddenly. Joe was jolted forward out of his seat. A bang came from the back of the van, and guns were fired at the front where the driver and second security guard were sitting.

The back door and the door next to Joe flew open. The keys jangled to the ground as he saw his father standing in front of him.

"Hello, Son." His father reached in and undid his cuffs and chains. Joe stepped out and they walked to a black car that was parked to the side of the prison van.

They both got in the front. Mr. Miller was driving.

"Where is Martin?" Joe asked.

"He died last week. Aine killed him in the courthouse," his father answered.

"What about Lindsey and Lacey?" Joe asked, looking around and noting that neither of them had been there to help his father.

"Both are gone, Joe. Orders from above," his father said.

Joe understood that they would not be too far behind if they failed.

"Where to?" Joe asked.

"We need to trace both Aine and Anchorette. Anchorette has left the country, and Aine is due to give evidence at your trial," Mr. Miller said, driving the car out of the city of London.

Lightning Source UK Ltd.
Milton Keynes UK
UKOW05f0030310714

236093UK00001B/151/P